MW01138449

FRIENDS LIKE THESE

A Love Like This 3

CARINA TAYLOR

CONTENTS

Dedication   v

1. Page   1
2. Noah   10
3. Page   17
4. Noah   28
5. Page   39
6. Noah   49
7. Page   60
8. Noah   70
9. Page   85
10. Noah   96
11. Page   103
12. Noah   111
13. Page   123
14. Noah   135
15. Page   145
16. Noah   165
17. Page   171
18. Noah   180
19. Page   186
20. Noah   190
21. Page   195
22. Noah   203
23. Page   209
Epilogue   220

The End   223
Acknowledgments   225
More from Carina Taylor: 227
Christmas Like This   229

THIS IS A WORK OF FICTION. NAMES, CHARACTERS, PLACES, AND INCIDENTS EITHER ARE THE PRODUCTS OF THE AUTHOR'S IMAGINATION OR ARE USED FICTITIOUSLY. ANY RESEMBLANCE TO ACTUAL PERSONS, LIVING OR DEAD, BUSINESSES, COMPANIES, EVENTS, OR LOCALES IS ENTIRELY COINCIDENTAL.

COPYRIGHT © 2020

ALL RIGHTS RESERVED. NO PORTION OF THIS BOOK MAY BE REPRODUCED IN ANY FORM WITHOUT PERMISSION FROM THE PUBLISHER, EXCEPT AS PERMITTED BY U.S. COPYRIGHT LAW.

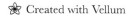 Created with Vellum

DEDICATION

This story is dedicated to my Grandpa Jim—the best snake storyteller there ever was.
I love you, Grandpa, and I can't wait to hug your neck when we meet in heaven.

Chapter One

PAGE

*H**elp!* *I've been kidnapped.*

Glancing around the half-full restaurant, I waited until no one was watching, then slipped the note into the waiter's hand.

A little water spilled from the pitcher he was pouring when our fingers touched. His eyes widened as he glanced down at the scrap of paper in his hand. I'd folded it so he couldn't read the words right away. He looked at me and winked. Too bad for him, it wasn't my phone number on the paper. I had standards—very few—and they included not dating high-schoolers.

"You're too young," I whispered. The waiter didn't appear to have heard me over the hum of voices and clinking of forks on plates.

"What was that you said?" The man sitting at my table glanced at me. I liked to call him kidnapper-number-one. His receding hairline was visible beneath his golfing cap as

1

he flipped through a *Golf Digest* magazine. He probably didn't fit the profile of most kidnappers.

"I said, wow, this is fun," I spoke up as I lifted my water glass in a salute.

With another wink, the waiter left me alone with my abductors.

"So, Page. Have you ever been golfing before?" Kidnapper-number-two asked me as she broke off a piece of bread and buttered it with a rounded knife.

I shook my head and grabbed a piece of bread for myself. I'd need to keep up my strength.

"It's okay if you're terrible at it at first. It's fun even then—especially for us." Kidnapper-number-one, a.k.a. Big Mike, a.k.a. my Uncle Mike chuckled at his joke.

They say that most kidnappings happen from someone you know. *They* were right.

Earlier that morning, Uncle Mike and Aunt Tricia asked my parents to go golfing with them. My parents already had plans, so they pointed my aunt and uncle in my direction.

Ever since Mike and Tricia had lost their daughter, the entire Boone family—including me—was unable to deny them anything. We wanted to do anything possible to help them through the grieving process. Their method of grieving consisted of taking up hobbies and spending quality time with family. That meant we tried to spend as much time with them as possible.

We'd made it past the badminton stage, thank goodness. Croquet was still on the way out. Golf was the most recent hobby they'd picked up, and they were excited to share the joy of it with the rest of us.

"You know, I was talking with the golf pro, Bob—he's our favorite—the other day, and he said I'd made phenomenal progress," Tricia explained in between bites of bread.

"That's wonderful, honey," Mike answered. "Page, why don't we get you started with a private lesson today?"

I coughed and took a sip of the tap water that tasted distinctly like chlorine. "Thanks, Uncle Mike, but I'd rather spend the afternoon learning from you."

Both Mike and Tricia sighed contentedly at that. Tricia looked at me out of the corner of her eye as she said, "You know, this course is a legend."

"That's so interesting." I smiled at them and took another sip of the water, not overly interested in learning about a golf legend. The course could be world renown, and I wouldn't know the difference from a backyard golf course.

A waitress delivered our sweet teas and lemonades, informing us there was a shift change, and she would be serving us for the rest of the meal.

I wrote a quick note on a napkin while she replenished our bread bowl.

Please start a grease fire for a distraction. I would rather do anything other than golf this afternoon.

Dropping the note in the waitress' apron pocket as she walked by, I glanced at the door that led to the kitchen. A man close to my age stood there, his hand resting on the door as he watched me. He was good looking, but prettier than me. I had a strict personal policy that I couldn't date someone prettier than me. He had blond hair, bright teeth, and looked like he belonged on the beach with a surfboard. Instead, he was in a restaurant wearing a suit sans tie. His smile stretched farther across his face as he studied me. The familiar way that he looked at me made me wonder if

I knew him. Maybe we went to school together. I never could remember faces.

I raised my eyebrows at him, then turned back to face the table. When I glanced over my shoulder a moment later, I watched him slip into the kitchen after the waitress.

By the time the waitress delivered the meal, I had built a house out of sugar packets on the table. Tricia and Mike had regaled me with golfing stories while we waited for our food. The waitress handed me a new napkin with a funny look on her face. I set the napkin in my lap before I opened it. There was a note written with permanent marker on the inside.

We regret that we can't start a fire to force an evacuation. Try faking a headache.

I looked up and found Blondie leaning against the kitchen doorway again, smiling at me. He rubbed his temples with exaggerated motions.

His antics almost made me smile, but a movement in the restaurant entrance caught my attention. A tall man wearing a suit and tie stood in the double-door entrance to the restaurant, talking on his phone. He appeared unconcerned about his location. His erect posture drew attention to his broad shoulders. His light brown, pompadour-styled hair looked as though it wouldn't dare move out of place. The man's face appeared determined as he spoke into the phone.

The electricity in the room seemed to intensify as he glanced through the restaurant, his eyes lighting on me for a moment—or maybe I imagined it. His handsome aquiline features should have given him the same pretty-boy look as Blondie, but the self-assured way he carried himself made it clear he was no boy.

A white-haired gentleman approached him, and the suit-man pocketed his phone while greeting the other man. As they stood there chatting, I found myself mesmerized by the handsome man. His arms were relaxed at his sides, but his body seemed coiled. Energetic. He was striking—not just his looks, but his entire carriage. I felt like I could reach out and touch him from where I sat. His presence made me forget about Blondie.

"Better tank up, trooper. We've got some golfing to do!" Mike drew my attention back to the table. When I glanced back over my shoulder, the suit-man was gone.

Picking up my fork, I took a bite of the tasteless food. Somehow the afternoon seemed duller now that the suit-man wasn't standing there where I could watch. It didn't make sense, but I hoped I would catch a glimpse of him again since we would be spending the afternoon at the golf course.

Even though I probably wouldn't see the man again, I knew that at least an afternoon playing golf would be more exciting than watching it.

I was wrong.

Watching golf on TV was not the most boring thing in the world: playing golf was.

I was grateful that I had escaped this specific torture for so long.

We'd made it to the ninth hole, and not without incident. I knocked over the contents of the golf bag—twice, lost ten golf balls, and hit the golf cart with my club. When I'd prepared to take a swing, I let go, and my club put a nice dent in the front of the golf cart.

I tried to rub it out like I would a wrinkle on my clothes except that wrinkle wouldn't fix. Aunt Tricia and Uncle Mike seemed to think it was hilarious while the caddy assured me it happened all the time—I didn't believe her.

Mike and Tricia stood a short distance away practicing their swings while I lay on my back in the grass. My golf club rested on my chest, and I hoped that I didn't become any fire ants' favorite afternoon snack.

It was a scorching fall afternoon in Louisiana—the worst time to be outside, in my opinion. My relatives were a special kind of crazy. They loved the hot and humid air. Me? Not so much.

I dreamed of Paris sidewalk cafes, a remote Italian vineyard, and quaint English towns. Instead, I lived in Louisiana. As a barista and starving artist, my finances weren't ready for a year-long European tour.

Even though I stashed away every penny possible, I still didn't have enough to quit my jobs and travel the world indefinitely. I'd been consoling myself with quick weekend trips. Usually I dragged my cousin, Jenny, with me. She was always game for quick trips. New York in three days? Possible. Skiing in Vale for a weekend? Also possible. I didn't know my legs could get that sore in such a short time. Jenny was in such good shape she didn't notice any difference. Over the years, I'd slowly been checking cities and sights off my list: Washington, D.C., The Grand Canyon, San Antonio, Los Angeles.

Someday I would tour Europe—right after I decided on a grown-up job that would provide a decent salary. Too bad I didn't know what I wanted to do for the rest of my life. There were too many options. How was a person supposed to decide anyway? They say to do what you love, so I'd looked into the possibility of becoming a professional cuddler. My cousin Kylie and her fiancé talked me out of it.

Tricia called out to me, interrupting my life review. "Paging Page!"

Never heard that before—at least not today.

I heaved myself off the ground and followed her: time to find that lost ball. It had landed near some tall grass on the edge of a pond. Although the rest of the golf course was meticulously maintained, the overgrown patch looked untouched. I'd heard of golf courses with sand traps, but I hadn't heard of miniature forests. My golf ball was somewhere in that thicket of grass. Traipsing through it wearing shorts did not sound pleasant.

"Page, here you go. You can start from the edge of the grass. This course is a legend for a reason, so I don't want you walking through the tall grass. We might be getting close to it," Tricia explained as she handed me another golf ball.

"Why won't you tell me about this so-called legend?" They'd been careful not to explain what it was. Maybe you had to be a club member to hear the story.

"You wouldn't have come with us if we told you!" Mike called from over by the golf cart.

They thought I wouldn't want to go golfing if they told me about the urban legend surrounding this golf course.

Newsflash: I didn't want to go golfing at all, but there I was anyway.

I bent down to place my eleventh golf ball on the ground. Tricia moved back to stand in the shade of the golf cart next to Mike. While I rested the golf ball on the tee, the tall grass in front of me shifted. It sounded like someone was walking through the grass—coming closer. My ears were playing tricks on me. Heatstroke was a real thing. Tricia had even warned me I should have drank more water.

I readjusted my grip on the golf club and made a few practice swings. The swishing sounded again, and I glanced around, trying to find the source of the noise.

I spotted two large beady eyes staring at me from the grass. A triangular head pointed straight at me. A long tongue flicked out, almost as if it was licking its chops while contemplating a snack.

It hadn't been a breeze that I heard.

The largest snake's head I had ever seen poked out of the thicket of grass, looking at me like I was lunch. It moved forward revealing part of a thick body.

My heart skipped a beat. My hands shook on the golf club grip.

Living in the south meant I'd seen my fair share of ugly, nasty snakes. I also had a healthy respect for them, thanks to the *incident*.

When my cousin Kylie and I were twelve, we fell into a cottonmouth nest. We'd been playing a game of sardines on Mimi's property with the rest of our cousins. We decided to hide together in the woods. When we ran down the hill towards the creek, we tumbled straight onto a nest. There was one mad momma plus lots of angry babies. Multiple bites later, and our parents had to rush us to the

ER. It left an impression and an allergy to the antivenom. Getting bit wasn't an option I liked to consider.

Shaking my head to clear away the bad memories, I tried to focus on the problem in front of me.

Trying to hit my golf ball and stay alive.

The snake opened its mouth wide, showing me the white inside that earned itself the cottonmouth nickname. I wanted to run, but all I could do was take a stumbling step back.

I heard Tricia gasp, and Mike said, "Good grief, it's true."

The snake slithered further onto the turf—straight toward me.

Chapter Two

NOAH

"I quit." The man slammed the door shut behind him as he left my office. His stomping footsteps echoed down the hall.

Pulling out my small day planner, I wrote a note to call the bookkeeper about the change in staff.

Sean Bartelli: send his last check to the provided mailing address.

I added a second note in the back of the book, reminding myself to ask more specific questions the next time I hired a golf pro.

The oak door opened for the second time in ten minutes. Kent, my golf course manager-in-training, stepped inside. He glanced out in the hall one more time before he closed the door. "What's Sean's problem?"

"He decided he didn't want to make a career here at The Garden. After one of our members complained about his golf lesson, I looked deeper into Sean's credentials. It turned out he was a tennis pro, not a golf pro. He forgot to mention that little detail in the interview. I asked him if it was a mistake; he got upset and quit. Saved me the breath it would have taken to fire him."

I brushed a hand over the top of my hair, careful to comb it in the right direction. Running a golf course was going to make me turn gray. It wasn't near as fun as my last business venture: opening a chain of cross fit gyms. Even starting a coffee shop from scratch and building a delivery business had nothing on trying to pull an unpopular golf course out of debt.

"Here's that updated list of members you wanted, along with the pending applications." Kent had found and organized the lists in less than an hour. That's why we worked well together. He was able to get things done, and I didn't have to micromanage him.

"And how is the guest policy coming along?" I asked him as I compared the handwritten guest list to the computer files.

"I've hired a copywriter to draft the terms."

"And the restaurant?"

He scrunched his face. "Horrible. The kitchen crew is slow, the customers are frustrated, and even a simple hamburger is tasteless."

"I know. Everything coming out of there is food that you can get at any old diner." I sighed and closed my laptop. I flipped open the day planner again to make another note.

Priority one: revamping the clubhouse restaurant.
   Email Xavier.

"What do you suggest for the restaurant?" I asked him. I'd already planned everything that needed to change, but was curious what Kent would suggest since he would be taking over management of The Garden soon.

"We need an entire new kitchen staff, new menus, and a facelift to the dining area. All things that cost more money, but the restaurant's a major part of this golf course. If we don't do any of that, we'll keep losing members to Sandy Pines."

My chest burned at the thought of losing our clientele to the neighboring golf course. Unfortunately, I couldn't exactly fault them for leaving The Garden. I had taken on the golf course precisely eight weeks before and was struggling to make it solvent again — lots of hiring and firing, with bankruptcy lurking around every corner.

"I've heard that Sandy Pines has French cuisine. I refuse to go find out for myself," Kent said.

Slipping my phone into my pocket, I walked to the large bay window that overlooked the golf course. I kept a pair of binoculars sitting on the windowsill for the days when I wanted to procrastinate on my real work.

My grandfather gave me a golf course that I didn't want so that he could "retire." While some might see this as a benevolent act on my grandfather's part, I knew the truth. My grandfather's 'gift' was the equivalent of giving me a sunken ship.

"What are we going to do about the Lucifer situation?" I asked Kent. Lucifer was another reason to be mad at my grandfather. I knew what we needed to do about the problem—I just wasn't sure how some of our members would feel about us moving him. They'd grown unhealthily attached.

Kent came to stand next to me, grabbed the binoculars off the windowsill and began scanning the golf course. "I don't know, sir."

"Please, I'm begging you, I'm not a sir. I'm thirty-two, not eighty."

"Alec insisted I call him sir when he was here. Old habits die hard."

"So does my grandfather," I muttered, though I didn't mean it. I didn't wish something terrible on my grandfather. I only wished that he was here to deal with the mess he created. Instead, he was wreaking havoc in other places in the world. And even though he was gone, he'd left behind his mascot, Lucifer.

"Look, she's napping." Kent chuckled, pointing out the window.

"Who's napping?" I squinted, but the figures were still blurry—time for some new contacts.

He grinned and passed me the binoculars. I scanned the area in the direction he'd been looking.

A woman lay flat on the green. I couldn't see her face since she had an arm over her eyes. Her golf club rested across her stomach. A caddy stood not too far away from her in the shade of the golf cart, guzzling a bottle of water. "Do you think she's hurt?"

"Nah, the relatives are right there with her. She's probably just getting a minor case of heatstroke. The heat index said it felt like one-hundred-and-eight today."

I glanced around with the binoculars and spotted a middle-aged couple teeing off, not twenty feet from the caddy. "Why do people golf at this time of day? Do we know her?"

"No, she's never been here before. She kept sending notes back to the kitchen today."

She must be pretty because Kent only remembered the pretty ones. "How do you know this? You don't wait on tables."

"I was checking on the kitchen staff when she was there eating lunch. She kept sending 'help' notes back to the kitchen staff, asking them to save her from a day of golf. I saved the notes. They were that good." He reached into his pocket and pulled out some paper napkins and handed them to me. I quickly read through them and couldn't help but chuckle.

"Make a note to switch the napkins to cloth instead of paper," I told him as I picked up the binoculars again. "How old is she?"

Kent waggled his eyebrows up and down. "Old enough."

"Not exactly what I meant." I set the binoculars down.

He flashed a grin before he turned toward my desk. "Well, beggars can't be choosers."

"You've dated three different women in four weeks. I don't think you qualify as a beggar."

"I think we're getting off-topic here, sir," he said, emphasizing the word 'sir' as he glared at me. "We were talking about the Lucifer situation."

I walked back to my desk and sat down, pulling a piece of cinnamon gum from a pack in my drawer. "You're the one who started talking about the girl."

"I couldn't help it. You should have stopped me and reminded me we were working."

"I'm not your babysitter. As long as you don't start dating members or staff, I don't care what you do." I opened my laptop and began researching restaurateurs. If I wanted a decent restaurant, I would have to hire someone who knew what they were doing. All the good chefs in New Orleans were already taken.

"Lucifer needs to go," Kent muttered as he scrolled through his phone.

Thank goodness I had another ally on that. "I agree." It was a liability waiting to happen. Golf courses shouldn't have mascots—especially ones like Lucifer.

Snakes weren't uncommon—Louisiana was full of

them. But The Garden was home for an eight-foot-long cottonmouth—and that *was* uncommon. It was an endangerment to the people on my course.

"Your grandfather will start a riot."

"He shouldn't have signed the golf course over to me then." I smiled, feeling genuine joy at the thought of removing Lucifer. My grandfather's obsession with that snake was unhealthy. He'd had it imported to the golf course from deep in the bayou—it was time to send the snake back.

Kent grinned. "Perfect. We'll take care of Lucifer this week."

I nodded. "I don't care if that snake is an urban legend. One of these days, it's going to bite someone. I don't know much about snakes, but something that big has got to have way more venom in a single bite."

Kent wandered back to the bay window and picked up the binoculars again. "They're all deadly if you wait too long to get the antivenom. Don't worry. I already compiled a list of snake re-locators. I'll have one of them come out early tomorrow morning."

"Sounds great," I said as I sent off an email to a friend of mine, Xavier Delgado, who was in the restaurant business. Hopefully, he'd be willing to give me a recommendation of a decent chef or restaurant manager—I'd take either one at this point.

"Holy..." Kent thumped his elbow against the window as he leaned closer to it.

Pressing a thumb against my forehead, I tried to rub some of the tension away. "What is it?"

"Lucifer's out."

"Give me those." I leaped out of my chair and yanked the binoculars from his hands. Kent still had the strap around his neck, and we each looked through a lens of the binoculars.

The girl who had been napping earlier was practicing her swing close to the marshy pond: Lucifer's pond.

Lucifer was coming out of the rushes and moving closer to the woman. She stopped her swinging but didn't run. Lucifer slithered closer. We'd never seen him get that close to someone before.

"Kent, call the hospital. If she gets bit, we're driving her directly there instead of waiting on an ambulance." I slipped the binoculars from around his neck and dropped them over mine.

"On it. What are you going to do?"

"I'm going down there to make sure nothing happens." I slammed open the office door and raced down the hall, running as fast as I could down the staircase and out the side door that led to the pro shop. I was regretting wearing my tailored suit—it didn't give me the range of motion that my gym shorts did. Leaping into a golf cart that one of my caddies was driving, I told him to floor it to Lucifer's Pit.

I focused my binoculars on the girl as we covered ground toward the ninth hole. The snake prepared to strike. Why didn't she run? She might have a chance if she got away from there.

The snake struck out at her.

I was too late.

Chapter Three

PAGE

"I'll take a video, Mike," Tricia whisper-yelled. "Page, don't worry. It hasn't bitten anyone. It's like a pet here. Don't be scared."

If my voice had been working, I would have told her I wasn't scared: I was terrified.

I stared at the biggest cottonmouth I'd ever seen. I stepped back with unsteady feet as the snake slithered out onto the grass. It was at least ten feet long—maybe fifteen, I couldn't be sure. It wouldn't even have to bite me—it could swallow me whole. Okay, maybe not, but I hated snakes. Size didn't matter. Big ones, small ones, I hated them all. It opened its mouth wide as if it was sizing me up to see if I'd fit. I should have eaten that second donut for breakfast.

With mouth stretched wide, it approached me. Knowing that cottonmouths like to scare people away with this tactic, I took a few steps backward, hoping the snake would stop following me. I did my best to move back with no abrupt movements.

They say snakes will leave you alone if you leave them

alone. I would gladly leave it alone. I would leave it alone so much it would be lonely.

But it continued to advance on me, not letting me put enough distance between us. It raised its head. Its body slithered after me while it poised its head like a spring.

You know the old fight-or-flight instinct?

Well, guess what? When you're facing off with a giant, poisonous cottonmouth that has lunch plans for you, those instincts kick in strong. Flight wasn't an option: I was so slow I didn't make it on the JV track team in high school.

Genetics made my choice for me.

The snake snapped its head back then struck forward at me. I leaped back, barely escaping its reach. It struck toward me a second time, and I jumped to the side, swinging my golf club with all of my strength.

The club connected with the snake's head, and the momentum knocked the snake several feet to the left. I stumbled over my own feet as I watched it convulse on its back. Finally, steadying myself, I turned and ran up the small slope.

If that monstrosity wasn't the devil in snake form, then I didn't know what was. It wouldn't surprise me if he rolled back onto his belly and slithered after me again.

I still couldn't believe I was fast enough to hit it before it bit me. If it had—but I didn't want to waste time dwelling on the possibilities of what could have happened—especially when those possibilities ended badly for me.

It was a miracle I had dodged two of his strikes before hitting him with the club. Once I was safe next to the golf cart, I turned and watched the writhing form on the grass, afraid to take my eyes off of it.

Uncle Mike patted my shoulder and chuckled. "You've got a killer swing."

His joking tone shattered my resolve to keep my legs firm.

"Hilarious. Excuse me while I pass out," I told him. The butterflies in my stomach started flying a figure-eight pattern while I stared at the shaking snake body. I was going to be sick. Uncle Mike wrapped an arm around my shoulders and turned me away.

"It's okay, kiddo. I'm glad you acted fast. That thing wanted to make a sandwich out of you. He sure was massive. I've never seen a snake that big. The rumors don't do it justice."

Tricia wrung her hands where she stood next to the golf cart. "I saw your life flash by, and all I could think is mercy, your momma would kill me if anything happened to you! I'm so glad you acted fast. I knew we should have told you about that legend. Of all the people to bring to the golf course with us, we shouldn't have let you near it."

I nodded as I tried to control my breathing once again. I hadn't been bitten. My heart was pumping steady—fast, but steady.

Several golfers gathered around to look at the now eerily-still snake. Then, the strangest thing happened. A wiry gentleman with thick, frameless glasses and an argyle vest stepped next to me. "Can I get your autograph? It will be worth some money someday."

He thrust a pen into my hand and passed me a crumpled receipt.

It looked like someone else was signing my name on the paper. The pen scribbled out my name while the man rambled on about me being a legend slayer.

Our caddy reached out and touched my arm. "Hey, I just wanted to say thanks. It's about time that happened." She shuddered as she looked at the snake. "I hated hanging around the ninth hole."

I glanced at the small crowd circled around us. I hadn't even noticed the people approach.

They all seemed to be snapping pictures. One man glared at me and loudly whispered, "Murderer!" I almost didn't hear what he said since his melting toupee distracted me.

Another middle-aged couple glared at me as they snapped a selfie with the dead snake in the background. They were still careful to keep a safe distance from it, I noticed.

A golf cart slid to a stop not three feet from me, distracting me from the picture takers. There was a bumper sticker slapped on the side that said *This is how I roll*. A man in a suit jumped out of the passenger side and ran to the snake.

My breath caught.

It was the same man I'd been watching just outside the restaurant entrance — the tall man who'd been on the phone.

"It's dead?" He demanded. Poor guy—he was probably as scared of snakes as I was. He stood there and stared at it. Like I was staring at him. Then he turned and locked eyes with me. I could see that his were steel blue— even across the turf.

He turned around to study the dead snake again, arms folded across his chest. The chatter died down around me, and my gaze fell to the snake at his feet.

My breath caught as the familiar wave of nausea swept over me: the pain, the swelling, the weakness in my limbs. The feelings I had experienced at twelve were washing over me as if I had been bitten again. The realization of how close I'd come to death was sinking in.

"She killed the legend. What are we going to do?" Someone whispered loudly.

The suit-man turned and locked eyes with me. He stepped between the snake and me, his sympathetic eyes searching mine. He gave me a reassuring nod. "It's dead."

I would have to marry him someday.

The murmurs from the small crowd continued buzzing around the air.

The man glanced at the picture-snapping people before he jabbed a finger in my direction and scowled.

"Come with me." The man exclaimed as he stalked toward me. His serious face looked as though it had been carved out of granite. Okay, I was rethinking my immediate marriage plans. I never handled angry people very well. I adjusted my grip on the golf club and brought it up to rest on my shoulder.

He stopped a few feet away.

I thought he might speak, but he glanced over my shoulder at the small audience and shut his mouth. He pointed at his golf cart that another caddy had just vacated. "Get in. We'll go talk at the office."

His low gravelly voice had me turning to follow him to the cart. I stopped next to it, realizing I was following a stranger and about to climb into a golf cart with him. I wouldn't be surprised if he pulled out a lollypop from his pocket and bribed me with it. Trust me, though; I'm not that easy. I wouldn't settle for anything less than a caramel apple pop.

"I'm sorry—who you are?"

His penetrating gaze seemed to see past my bravado. His straight nose and chiseled jaw were almost too perfect —no defect in sight.

"I own the golf course," he bit out.

That would explain why I didn't know who he was. I'd never heard of this golf course until Tricia and Mike had dragged me here. If it hadn't been for them, I wouldn't be standing here with an angry, good-looking guy who was ordering me into a golf cart.

Not that I was upset about the good-looking part. I wasn't. But since the guy looked like he wanted to run me over with said golf cart, that negated the handsome part.

I glanced back at Tricia. She jerked her head like she was trying to tell me to get in the golf cart. She mouthed, "Go with him."

"Get in," the man said as he looked back at the small crowd.

I hopped in. My butt barely hit the leather seat before he took off. It would have been a lot more dramatic if it hadn't been an electric golf cart. Peeling out on a golf course without a single sound, dramatically lowers your tough-guy persona.

"You've never been here before," he commented.

"There are lots of places I've never been."

He didn't reply. He kept facing forward as he drove faster over the course. He must have installed some nitrous oxide on the cart.

The silence was killing me. I wanted to find a relevant topic that would make this drive less awkward—and distract me from staring at him. "Do you have big plans for Halloween this year? It's not that far away. I've been planning my outfit for my family's party for a while now."

Yes, smooth conversation starter, Page. He'll definitely think you're charming after that lead-up.

He glanced at me, looking mildly less angry.

I kept talking—babbling, really. "What are you going as? No, don't tell me. I'll guess. I'm good at this game."

I turned in the leather seat so that I could study him. Really, it was just an excuse to stare at him openly. His jaw was clean-shaven, but I could see a shadow appearing. He probably had to shave every morning—maybe even twice a day. We hit a bump, and his hand shot out to grab my shoulder and steady me before I could fall out of the cart backward.

"Captain America. You're planning on dressing up as Captain America. I'd almost place money on that."

"Wrong," he said, but his lips quirked to the side. Maybe I was close to the truth.

"Good thing I didn't put any money down. I'll figure it out."

"I'm not—"

"It has to be Thor," I interrupted him. "Maybe Batman. We have our annual harvest party coming up; you should come. It will be so great. There's a contest for best dressed. Mimi always wins, so I'm convinced she's rigged the system or bribed the judges."

Suit-man jerked the cart to the right, narrowly avoiding a bird flying by. "You realize Halloween is still weeks away, right?"

"When you're competing for best dressed against your grandmother, it's never too early to plan."

He smiled at that, and it was a friendly smile. "Tough competition."

When he parked outside the clubhouse, he motioned for me to follow him with a crook of his finger.

I figured I should text Mom and let her know where to look for my body in case this man murdered me. He'd probably do it with his index finger too. It was always the good-looking ones who were serial killers.

He led the way into the clubhouse, and I followed as I texted my mom. I didn't pay attention to where we were going—there were definitely some stairs involved—until he halted in front of a door. I stopped too—right after my face slammed into his back. He turned around and narrowed his eyes at me before he opened the door to an office.

I held up my phone. "Sorry, I just wanted to let someone know who to look for when the police find my body in a dumpster. What's your name?"

"Noah Dunaway." His eyebrows flew up, and his lips twitched before he stepped inside the office and held the door open for me. "Overactive imagination much?"

"Possibly." I stepped inside and glanced around the office. It reminded me of my grandma: lots of leather and not a thing out of place. The only thing it was missing was the scent of tobacco. That was no surprise. This clean-shaven man probably believed caffeine was a drug, and that sweets were of the devil—he definitely wouldn't poison his body with nicotine.

He closed the door, careful not to slam it. Now that I was in an enclosed space with him, he didn't seem as severe as he did on the golf course. Serious, maybe, but not angry.

He sat down in a large leather chair behind a mahogany desk. He steepled his fingers and pressed them against his lips. The large office grew infinitesimally smaller with his undivided attention focused on me.

I don't know why I followed him here. The only reason I could think of was curiosity. His fierceness had distracted me from a panic attack. When he stepped in front of the snake, I imagined it was to protect me from the gruesome sight. He'd probably been unaware of where he stood, but a girl could dream.

"You've ruined me," he said in a voice so quiet I almost couldn't hear him over my heavy breathing.

I scooted closer to the door. If he was talking to me, then he was still angry. If he was talking to himself, that meant he was crazy. Neither were nice options.

Now that I thought about it, there was also the distinct possibility that when he was stepping between the snake and me, he was doing it to protect the snake from *me*, and not as a gentlemanly gesture.

His solemn gaze focused on me again.

I shifted from foot to foot. It was the perfect time to do one of the oldest and wisest traditions that had failed me earlier: run.

"Don't." His voice stopped me mid-step as I headed for the door. "The people will be out there still. They were upset."

The small crowd *had* seemed a little uneasy...

His voice softened when he spoke again, "Do you know why this golf course has become so popular in the past couple of months?"

I straightened my shoulders and stepped closer to his desk, curious why he would ask me such a question. "Let me guess; you have a great marketing team?"

He blinked slowly at me, and I watched as a bead of sweat rolled down his temple. He stood and slid his suit jacket off, hanging it over his chair before he sat down again.

I watched the whole thing. His fitted shirt showed that he did more than sit behind a desk all day. The sleeves pulled tight against his biceps, making me want to run my hands over them.

"My marketing team sucks." His words put a halt to my admiration. Right. We were talking about the golf course.

"Well, maybe you should look for someone more qualified if you want a legendary golf course."

He pinched the bridge of his nose, hiding his facial expression behind his large hand. "You killed the only marketing tool I had."

I looked at him blankly. He and I must have been on different wavelengths because I was pretty sure the world's biggest snake just tried to kill me. I couldn't quite figure out how it was involved with his marketing plan.

"How exactly?"

He narrowed his eyes at me then pointed at the chair across from his desk. He didn't say a word, simply pointed, like I was a well-trained puppy. I sat in the chair next to the window instead.

"Lucifer—the snake—"

"Yes, I assumed that's who you were talking about."

His lips pressed tightly together as he glared at me. "Do you mind? As I was saying, Lucifer brought in business regularly. He brought me far more business than my marketing team ever did. And now he's gone."

This man seemed a little put out about me taking care of his golf course's little snake problem. I thought he would have been a little grateful. But it seemed like he was only worried about his revenue. I clenched my fist at my side, reminding myself that I couldn't treat him the same as I would an eight-foot cottonmouth.

"Don't take this the wrong way, but have you seen your psychiatrist this week?" I asked him because, apparently, I didn't know when to keep my mouth shut.

His eyes widened, and I could see the pulse stand out on his neck. I brushed a drop of sweat from my cheek.

He stood up, and I scooted to the edge of my seat while mentally measuring the distance to the door.

He reached under his desk, and I heard a drawer or cupboard open. Then, he walked over to me and handed me a cold sparkling water.

"It's hot out there today." He gave me a small smile as I took the cold glass bottle from him. I pressed it to my cheek before I opened it and took a drink. He continued saying, "I'm sorry. I should have offered you something right away. You were out in the sun and then had the scare of your life. You're probably dying of thirst."

He didn't seem like he was mad at me at all. Maybe I'd misread him.

I had been known to be wrong a time or two in my life.

Chapter Four

NOAH

I rubbed a hand over my face as I tried to decide what to do with the woman sitting in my office. I understood what Kent meant now. She was funny, spunky, and a nervous talker. When she started rambling on our ride back to the clubhouse, I knew right away that I liked her. Most people were careful to hide their nervousness, but not her. Everything about her was sincere.

"What's your name?"

"Page Boone." She shifted in her seat and glanced around the office. Her eyes took in every detail.

"How did you get here?"

Her eyes settled on me, and she pursed her lips. "Well, my parents loved each other very much—and when two people love each other—"

I started choking on air, something I didn't even know was possible.

She smirked at me, and I had a feeling she enjoyed keeping people uncomfortable.

From what I gathered from her defensive posture earlier, I made her nervous. That was the last thing I wanted to do. Then again…she wanted to make me uncomfortable? Two could play that game.

Never mind that she solved all of our problems with one good swing, I just wanted to see her reaction if I gave her a hard time about it. "What brought you to The Garden today?"

"Actually, my aunt and uncle brought me. I tried to get out of it, but the restaurant staff wasn't very helpful."

"So, you didn't even want to be here, but you killed our mascot anyway?"

"Never come between a woman and her golf ball. He was blocking me out. How was I supposed to beat Uncle Mike if I didn't hit it? It was like forty-luv." The tremor in her jaw gave away her bravado. I sighed and pressed a hand against my mouth to hide my smile.

I shook my head at her scorekeeping. What was with people thinking golf and tennis were interchangeable?

Note to self: teach her a few basics about golf.

"What made that snake follow after you like that? He's never come out of the rushes after anyone before."

"He probably liked my perfume." She pointed at the binoculars that were still hanging around my neck. "Wait, how did you know he came out after me? Were you spying on me? Because that's what it sounds like."

I shrugged, feeling my cheeks warm. It wasn't like I stood there watching out the window all day long. "Every once in a while, I look out there to make sure everything is okay."

She sighed. "This is too sad."

"Why is it sad?"

"You must live a boring life. No adventure. You can only live vicariously through other people—who golf." She swiped at a few fake tears and motioned to the binoculars.

"You have to watch through your big fancy window to have any excitement."

I fought another smile as I told her, "I promise I do not lack adventure."

Leaning forward on my desk, I straightened the papers Kent had brought me earlier. When I pulled up next to Lucifer's pit, the small crowd had already been whispering words about her. They had been upset she killed the legend.

She had been justifiably frightened after facing Lucifer, and the last thing she needed was to have people be angry at her. I wanted to keep her away from the crowds of people trying to talk to the 'legend slayer.' The term had already gained momentum by the time I reached her. She would either become the next novelty at the golf course, or people would be irrationally angry that she had acted out in self-defense.

"Prove it," she demanded.

"Prove what?"

"That you live an adventurous life!"

"I don't have to prove it."

She laughed. "That means you don't live an adventurous life."

"Why does it feel like I'm on the school playground again getting dared to do something?"

She leaned forward and rested her elbow on the arm of her chair. "Does it work to dare you? Because I'm curious what a golf course owner does for an adventure."

"Maybe running a golf course is an adventure."

"Not sure that counts. Maybe with that snake living on the course." She shuddered even though she was the one who mentioned it. Most people feared snakes—Page was no exception. She'd probably be especially scared of them after Lucifer.

Time to keep her distracted with an argument until Kent let me know the coast was clear for her to leave. "That snake was an attraction for people."

Her face relaxed, and she leaned back in her chair. "So was the guillotine. Not all attractions are good attractions."

I couldn't agree more.

But it was fun to play devil's advocate for once. Usually Kent took on that role. "Lucifer brought a third of our golfers here to The Garden."

She walked around to my side of the desk and patted my shoulder like we were old friends. I froze—afraid that if I moved, she'd pull her hand away. "Don't worry; we'll find you something else that will bring in customers. I'll help."

The serious look in her eye made me sit up straight. "What do you mean 'you'll help?'"

"I'm fantastic at coming up with unique ideas. It's pretty much my specialty." She smiled at me, and I thought about what it would be like to kiss those heart-shaped lips.

"You realize you're probably a YouTube sensation by now."

Her lips quirked to the side. "Unfortunately, that's not how I wanted to become famous."

Leaning forward, I rapped my knuckled on the desk as I looked up at her. "Oh, so you're looking to become famous?"

"Well, I do dabble in art." She grazed her fingers along the edge of my chair.

I took a steadying breath before I asked, "What type of art?"

"Watercolor. Oils. Sketching. Sculpting is still an elusive skill."

"You're an artist?" That was a large variety of skills for one person. I wondered if she was any good.

"Trying to be."

31

She picked up my mug and glanced at the now-cold tea inside of it. She scowled. I snatched the cup out of her hand and set it down beyond her reach.

"What do you like to paint?"

"I've just finished a collection of Picasso imitations. I think you need one on your wall." She pointed to the blank space on the wall where I had removed some of my grandfather's tasteless art.

"You'll have to show me your paintings sometime. I have been looking for a piece to hang there. It seems a little empty in here without something."

"I'd like to give you one," she said as she sat on my desk. I had chairs all over my office, but she chose to sit on top of my papers.

My phone rang, interrupting me from accepting the offered painting sight-unseen. I studied her as I answered it. "Hello?"

Page swiped a finger over the top of my computer monitor then held it out to me as though she were the dust police.

I swiped the dust off of her finger with the sleeve of my shirt while I listened to my restaurant supplier tell me why their rates were increasing. "Look, you told me if we went with you as a supplier, you would give us a price guarantee for a year. It's been four weeks. I have it in the contract that you'll be meeting those prices for the next eleven months."

"Manufacturing prices have risen, and we can't cover costs if we continue selling at that price. We'd go bankrupt supplying to you at the price we are right now," the whiny voice on the other end of the phone told me.

With a groan, I tapped a hand against my desk. "I'll be looking over our contract carefully, and you had better be prepared to honor it."

I hung up the phone and noticed Page held last week's guest book on her lap and was flipping through it, looking at the signatures. "You have a few regulars, but nobody steady."

"That seems to be the consensus." I gritted my teeth together.

She glanced up sharply. "Problems in paradise? Is that why you were so worried about losing the snake?"

Her hazel eyes studied mine, and even though I had an excuse on the tip of my tongue, I told her the truth. She had no vested interest in this golf course—especially after Lucifer tried to eat her for lunch. "The course is having some issues right now. I took over eight weeks ago, and I'm discovering problem after problem."

She nodded and turned back to the guest book. "You'll straighten it out. I can tell."

Her words made me want to puff out my chest like a professional weightlifter. Her opinion mattered more than it should.

But she wasn't the person I wanted to complain about work troubles with—I wanted to impress her, not scare her away. "Are you all right? It's not every day a person comes face to face with an eight-foot cottonmouth."

She lifted her head and her eyes locked on mine. My breath caught as she leaned closer to me and spoke in a soft voice. "You're worried about me."

Right then, the office door slammed open, and Kent walked into the room, interrupting our moment. He stopped short when he saw Page sitting on my desk leaning toward me. "Oh, hello."

She tilted her head toward him. "Hey! Blondie. You're the one who kept sending me notes at the table. You weren't very helpful."

She raised her eyebrows at Kent, and suddenly I felt a

twinge. A twinge of something almost like jealousy. Sure, she hadn't smiled at him, but she was paying more attention to him than me now.

Kent smiled what I liked to call his 'sleaze' smile. The one he smiled whenever he was trying to impress a girl. He was usually good at it, too.

"What is it, Kent?" I bit out.

"Everyone's downstairs. They didn't leave. Instead, they decided to talk about Lucifer in the airconditioned restaurant. I think they're starting a memorial service for him right now. The staff is swamped."

Great. Just what I needed today—a snake funeral. "You couldn't handle it?"

"They're short-staffed—it will probably take both of us."

"Wonderful." It was not wonderful. I didn't want to deal with my incompetent restaurant staff right then. I wanted to keep talking with Page. Unfortunately, reality was calling. The price of owning a business—I had no time to call my own.

"I'll be back in a moment," I told Page. I grabbed my jacket off the chair and was surprised when two slender hands helped me slide it on. She stepped in front of me and helped straighten it before she buttoned the front. I stood there, mesmerized by her touch.

"There, now you look like a professional." She patted my chest, her pale blue fingernails contrasting against my dark navy suit. I wondered if she could feel my heart thundering under her hand.

I cleared my throat. "Thank you." With a reluctant dip of my head, I walked around her and out the office door. I glanced over my shoulder—she was smiling at me.

Kent gave me a funny look when I followed him down the hall. "So, that's the way it is," he said quietly.

"I don't know what you're talking about." I brushed some imaginary lint off of my arms.

He snorted but didn't say another word until we reached the restaurant. "We're short on wait staff today, and the main grilling element went out. The cook doesn't know how to make anything without that grill."

"We need a new chef," I complained. "And more reliable wait staff."

"Yes, to both those things."

We stepped through the restaurant doors. Every table was full, and there were only two waiters in sight. Several hands waved through the air, trying to get their attention.

"What in the world?"

It looked like every golfer who'd ever been to The Garden now sat in my restaurant.

"I told you. The golfers are all here to toast Lucifer." Kent grumbled. "It would have been better if I could quietly remove him from the course. But no, several people got a full video of her killing that snake."

Someone tapped their glass where they stood on the small stage designed for live music—which we never had.

"Excuse me!" He was an older gentleman who was one of my grandfather's friends. I recognized the man right away. He routinely complained about anything and everything when he was at The Garden. Clearing his throat, he began his speech. "Today is a sad day for us all. A fine specimen killed in the prime of its life. We looked forward to any chance we had to see Lucifer—"

"Please tell me I didn't walk in during a snake eulogy," a soft voice whispered.

I spun around to find Page standing to my left. "That's what it is all right. Come with us; they might start a riot if they see you."

I held out a hand, motioning for her to follow Kent and

me. She surprised me by grabbing my hand. I didn't let go as we made our way around the outside of the room, heading for the kitchen. I pushed open the swinging door and stepped inside.

Voices yelled back and forth, smoke and steam filled the room, and I think one of my waiters was crying.

"This is bad," Page commented unnecessarily.

"Want me to announce that the restaurant is closed?" Kent asked.

I felt, more than saw, Page's eyes on me. I stepped forward into the middle of the chaos and spoke to the chef. "Tell me what's going on."

Everyone started yelling at once.

Holding up my left hand since Page still held my right, I added, "One at a time."

Layton, the college student who we hired on for the fall, started. "Karissa and Benson didn't come in for their shift today, and Colin's out sick. It's only Tammy and me. We can't keep up on the orders and bus the tables."

I nodded then turned to Reggie, the cook. "What's going on, Reggie?"

"Brent had a court date today, and Gene called in sick, too, so it's only me. The grill quit working, and Layton set a plastic tote on the hot stovetop. It melted over everything. I have nothing to cook on until we fix the grill and clean the stove."

I wondered what Brent had had a court date for since he hadn't bothered to mention it to me, but I kept that thought to myself. "The plastic tote explains that awful smell. You can't cook anything without the grill?"

Reggie shook his head.

Page squeezed my hand, then pulled away. She marched to the sink, scrubbed her hands and arms, then jerked an apron off the peg on the wall and pulled it over her head. She grabbed an extra golf cap from the top of a shelf and slipped it on, tugging her ponytail out the backside and yanking the cap low over her forehead.

I continued watching her as I debated what to do. She snatched a menu off of the small shelf that held extras. She backed up to me and asked, "Mind tying this up for me?"

Since I still couldn't figure out what she was doing, I grabbed the apron strings and tied it in a neat bow around her waist while she studied the menu.

"Hey, you!" She called to Reggie, the chef—if we could call him that. "Are you set for salads?"

He looked at her with a stunned expression but nodded.

"Good." She pointed to the two servers standing on the other side of the counter looking ready to hide in the cooler. "You two, we're pushing salads. If anyone asks, it's Heart Healthy Awareness Day, and if anyone asks for a burger or something else fried, point them back to the salad menu. Tell them it's in honor of Lucifer's memory if you have to."

"What if they give you a hard time?" I asked. "It's a funeral for the snake you killed."

She shrugged. "I'll pour water and bus tables. Hopefully they won't notice me."

She scooped up a freshly poured water pitcher in one hand, and a salad menu in the other then disappeared into the restaurant.

"That was—wow," Kent said as he stared after her.

"Devious. Brilliant. Commandeering. A bit tyrannical," I said with a smile.

"I want to ask her out, but now I'm oddly terrified of her," Kent mused.

I glared at him. "If anyone's going to ask her out, it's going to be me."

He groaned. I removed my jacket and rolled up my shirt sleeves. After washing my hands, I slipped on an apron and tossed another to Kent. "We're serving today. And we'd better have some new potential hires here in the morning, or this is what you'll be doing for the foreseeable future."

I grabbed a salad menu off the shelf and a warm carafe of coffee.

Time to salvage the afternoon.

Chapter Five

PAGE

"Thank you." Noah's low voice rumbled behind me. "You didn't have to help us like that, especially after everything that happened to you on the course today."

We had finished serving the snake mourners, and Noah had closed the restaurant two hours early. I turned around from where I stood in the front lobby of The Garden. "You know, you almost sound like you're feeling sorry about it, even though I killed your main attraction."

He nodded slowly. "I thought I would have a heart attack when Lucifer struck out at you."

He was worried about me even though I'd killed his pet. It was sweet and selfless of him. "Thank you for getting me away from the snake earlier. It was making me sick looking at it."

"Of course, I understand."

I swayed back and forth as I studied Noah's smile—even that was perfect. "Well, I'd better go find Tricia and Mike."

"The couple you were golfing with?"

"Yes. They're my ride home."

"They left."

I shook my head. Leave it to Tricia and Mike to forget that I rode with them. I should have flown to Chicago on my days off, except then I would have missed meeting Noah.

Okay, I was glad I hadn't gone to Chicago this week. But that still meant I needed to figure out how to get home. Ten minutes away by car, but I didn't want to pay for an Uber. Three miles wasn't that far. When I visited New York City, I walked everywhere to save on taxi fare. I'm sure I could walk three miles in under an hour.

"Good luck with your golf course. I'm sorry about killing your mascot. I'm not sorry for the snake, but I am sorry for you."

He smiled at that. "Thank you."

Reluctantly looking away from his face, I turned to leave.

He stopped me. "Wait, do you have a ride?"

"No, but it's not far."

He took a step towards me. The soft scent of cinnamon enveloped him. He shoved his hands into his pants' pockets and asked, "How far is not far?"

"Only three or four...miles," I whispered the last bit.

He frowned and dug around in his pockets. "You're not walking that far in this heat by yourself. I'll drive you." His eyes flashed as he searched my face. "Unless you don't trust me. In that case, I'll order you an Uber."

I bit my lip. "I trust you. Besides, I texted my mom your name, remember?"

He grinned at that. "I remember."

He pulled his keys out of his pocket and opened the door for me.

"Noah!"

We both turned to see Kent rushing into the lobby. "The lawyer is here. He said he had more paperwork for you to sign."

Noah muttered under his breath. "I'd forgotten about our appointment. It has to be today?"

He looked at me while Kent answered him, "Yes, it's the last part of the transfer."

Noah regarded my face for a moment, then sighed and tossed his keys to Kent. "Here. Page needs a ride home. You can take my car." He turned back to me and said in a low voice, "I'm sorry I can't drive you home. But I hope I'll see you again. Soon."

He smiled, and his eyes sparkled when I smiled back. The energy between us was real—not something I imagined. We would see each other again; I'd make sure of it. Hopefully, it wouldn't involve golfing or snakes the next time.

I followed Kent out to the parking lot, mildly—greatly—upset that Noah wouldn't be the one taking me home.

Once Kent and I sat in Noah's car, I told him the general direction of my house, then turned the air conditioner up and looked out the window at the passing scenery. Something bumped my seat. Kent's hand rested on my headrest. "Shoulder problems?"

He just smiled. I'm sure he thought it was a charming smile. It wasn't—not to me, not compared to Noah's genuine and unpracticed smile.

"So, have you lived in Charlesville long?" he asked as he glanced between me and the road.

"Yes..."

"You go into Nola much?"

I shrugged. "Do you need directions?"

His fingers brushed the back of my neck. I felt nothing.

Maybe a faint chill. Not like the electric current I'd felt when I held Noah's hand earlier.

"Whatever it is you think you're doing—it's not working."

He scowled, but quickly smoothed his face into a smile again. "I'm not trying to do anything."

I glared at him. "Good, because you don't stand a chance."

He tapped a finger against my shoulder. "Are you sure? Because I can be a lot of fun."

"Not to me." I reached behind my head and grabbed his wrist, then shoved it back towards him. "Listen, Clark."

"It's Kent."

"Whatever. Your lines might work on someone else, but I've been fed every line there ever was. Heck, I might even invented some lines myself, so no. I'll pass on letting you 'show me Nola.'"

He stared straight ahead with a grim set to his mouth.

"Where did I go wrong?" He asked as he pulled to a stop in front of my house. "Usually, my game's pretty good."

I grabbed the door handle but then answered him before I got out. "First off, Noah caught my attention first. I'm not interested in anyone else now. Second, you're a creep when you touch someone's neck and shoulders. Reminds me of a reptile, and I have a bad history with those."

He glared at me. "Why don't you tell me how you really feel?"

"Oh, okay, I—"

"Never mind, get out."

I grinned and jumped from the car. "Thanks for the ride, Clark!"

I hurried down the path that led to my house in the

backyard. Kent wasn't a creep. Sleazy, but not creepy. He just needed to be knocked down a few pegs and I didn't mind doing it. Who knows, maybe someday he'd thank me for it.

That evening I sat down at my desk to sketch. I hadn't planned what I was going to draw. Instead, I sat there with a pencil in hand as I reminisced about the events of the day.

My hand decided to sketch Noah.

After nearly being eaten by a snake that was longer than my car, I thought I'd be a little more consumed with terror. Instead, I was too busy thinking about the golf course owner with a twinkle in his eye. He'd seemed so serious as we talked in his office. Then I realized he was being sweet and trying to keep me away from the crazy people. He seemed so proper—and in need of some loosening up. Once he'd relaxed around me, he started smiling more and more. I knew he needed more of that.

When he'd explained about the trouble with the golf course and gaining new members, I knew he needed help. He didn't seem like the over-sharing kind—unlike me—so it felt even more special that he'd opened up to me. While he hadn't said it in so many words, I knew he was in trouble.

I had killed his only attraction. While I didn't feel bad for defending myself, I felt terrible that I had taken away the one thing that brought new business to the golf course. I didn't agree with Noah's business model because there had to be better ways to attract members than a snake. Maybe he just needed to take one of those online courses that taught you everything you needed to know about marketing in thirty-minutes. It'd probably be beneficial to him. I'd have to tell him next time I saw him.

I wasn't looking forward to mentioning the snake again. Noah seemed to be soft-hearted. He'd seemed a little distraught at the snake's death. The way he'd been rubbing his face—almost as though he were holding back tears.

I wanted to make it all better for him.

The restaurant crisis had sealed the deal. The way he had treated his staff kindly even in the midst of a stressful situation had revealed all I needed to know about his character. He hadn't yelled at his incompetent staff. He hadn't passed the blame to everyone around him. He hadn't strangled Kent for not fixing the problem. He'd shown far more self-control in that situation than I would have. *He* was the reason I wanted to help.

When he stepped out of the kitchen with rolled-up shirtsleeves wearing an apron and carrying a coffee carafe, I had asked myself, had anyone ever looked that good before? Probably not. His piercing blue eyes, styled hair, and muscled forearms were a lethal combination. The apron stretched against his chest—as if it were big enough to protect his crisp white shirt from a stain or splatter.

As we served the overfilled dining hall, no one made the connection that I was the girl who killed the snake. I had pulled that cap low over my eyes; it was a wonder I didn't spill anything.

Noah was careful to steer me away from a few people in the room—the ones who seemed the most upset about Lucifer dying. Noah took the plates from me anytime we got close to the table where the eulogist sat. He told me he didn't want me to have to face him that day after everything. I thought it was strangely sweet and protective.

Which brought me to a conclusion: I was going to help Noah. A guy like him deserved to succeed.

I propped my sketch of him next to my family photo, his strong jaw a prominent feature in the drawing.

I wouldn't mind looking at that every day.

Now, all I had to do was figure out how to bring more business to Noah's golf course. Luckily, I had the perfect cousin to call. My cousin Kylie worked for a marketing company called SV Marketing in Lampton, which was only an hour from me. She would have excellent marketing advice.

I pulled my phone out of my pocket, set it on speakerphone, and placed it on the table next to my pencils. It rang while I organized my paint supplies.

"Hello?" A woman answered the phone.

"Hey, Kylie! How's Hagen?" I asked.

"I'm doing great, thanks so much for checking up on me instead of my fiancé," she complained.

"Ah, well, I know you're fine. I only wanted to know if you'd shoved him in your garbage can yet."

"Not yet, but he's almost finished building my pergola, so he might outlive his usefulness."

I grinned. Kylie was the nicest of us Boone's. The mothering cousin: she would feed you, take care of you, encourage you, and was generally more responsible than the rest of us. That is...until she met her fiancé. She'd gone full Boone on him in an all-out prank war.

"So, I was calling to ask you about some marketing techniques."

"Oh no, what are you up to now?" She groaned.

"What do you mean? Why do I have to be up to something?"

"Are you trying to sell your paintings again?"

"No, nobody seems to like my Picasso replications." Not that I tried that hard.

"That's okay; you're very talented at other things."

"Besides, I'm saving all of those to give to you and Hagen when you get married."

Something crashed on her end of the line. I could hear her voice call farther from the phone. "Hagen! She's trying to give us her Picasso paintings."

I heard a deep voice in the background answer her. "Oh no, not that. Let's change our names and move out of the country."

"Hilarious, you guys, I can hear you," I yelled, even though I knew to expect Hagen's teasing. He could hold his own with the Boone family but was sweet to Kylie, which was why I liked the guy.

"Okay, okay," Kylie spoke into the phone again. "What's the problem? Tell me everything. Hagen went back outside to barbecue."

Clearing my throat, I lined up my paintbrushes in size order on the desk. "Say that there was a struggling business. Just as a random example—an unsuspecting soul accidentally destroyed the only thing that drew in new customers. What would you do?"

"Wait, that made zero sense. Why don't you go ahead and tell me what you did?"

I sighed. I guess there wouldn't be any way to avoid

telling her the whole story. After making her promise not to tell Hagen, I told her the story about going golfing with Aunt Tricia and Uncle Mike, including killing the snake and meeting Noah.

"I've heard about that golf course. Dave, my neighbor, told me about it."

"So, are you saying I killed any chance for a successful golf course?"

"No, it's just that's the way it's known. One of the best marketing techniques is to have something unique. An experience you can't get anywhere else. I'll admit, using an oversized cottonmouth is unconventional, dangerous, and the worst idea ever, but it seemed to work. I don't golf, but even I've heard of The Garden."

I was the worst person in the world. Noah's golf course really was in trouble because of me.

"Maybe we could find him an Adam and Eve instead of a Lucifer."

Kylie laughed. "Please, don't be Eve."

"I won't, but Noah would make a great-looking Adam."

"I think you should just let it go, Page. There was nothing else you could have done."

"Oh, there wasn't? Why didn't I run? Why didn't I pay attention to my surroundings and the fact I got close to that tall patch of reeds? What if the snake wasn't trying to kill me, and it was just trying to get to the grass to sun itself?"

"You're going to make me have to repeat myself, aren't you? There was nothing else you could have done. You were out of options. You could have let that snake bite you, but then you'd be dead. Stop blaming yourself and find a way to move past this. Now, I've got to take some muffins to Dave before Hagen finds them and eats them all."

"Thanks for the help—and the pep talk. Love you."

"Love you, too. Talk to you later."

I hung up the phone and flopped on my bed. My small cottage had an open floor plan, making it easy to stare at the sketch of Noah that sat on my desk. I didn't want to paint—I wanted to lay there and think about how to make this up to Noah.

Kylie had told me to stop blaming myself and move past this. How did I move past it when I knew I'd doomed Noah's whole business? He so calmly dealt with the situation in the kitchen, not once getting mad. He was so good at getting me off the golf course when a crowd had gathered. He didn't even lose his temper when he found out half of his staff didn't show up.

I was mad for him. He shouldn't have to put up with any of that. Too many things went wrong that day. A missing chef and wait staff? A broken grill? Someone incites a snake eulogy? Lame excuses for not coming to work? How much bad luck could a guy have? Bad luck or not, I was going to bring him only good luck from then on out.

It was time to brainstorm.

Chapter Six

NOAH

Opening the window to let in fresh air before the weather grew hot for the afternoon, I turned around to find Kent standing just inside my office door. We'd just finished interviewing candidates for the wait staff and had hired two more servers. I was still waiting to hear back if I got the chef I wanted. After reading my email, Xavier knew of someone right away and put me in touch with the guy. Kent had already found a real golf pro who would come in for an interview the next week.

Things were looking up.

"Page dropped something off for you. She said she didn't want to have a guilty conscience, and so she found the perfect mascot for you."

Page had stopped by. It had been three whole days since the Lucifer incident.

I couldn't believe I'd missed her. While I couldn't exactly sit at the reception desk just waiting for her, someone should have told me.

"Why are you grinning? What did she bring?"

"She brought you a mascot. It's in my office. She

wanted to be here when you saw it, but she had to head to work."

He was still grinning, which made me suspicious. Kent grinned more than a person should. He was all around too smiley. You can't trust a person who smiles that much. It made me confident of one thing: whatever Page had left behind for me, probably wasn't a goldfish.

"Just tell me what it is."

He grinned and shook his head. "Follow me."

I followed him downstairs to the back hallway where his office was located. I needed to see about moving it upstairs. His office was too far away—it was getting annoying having to run downstairs or upstairs every time we needed to bring each other something.

I was a little terrified to find out what Page's idea of a golf course mascot was. Hopefully not the same as my grandfather's. I didn't need another fatal attraction.

"Here, she left you a note." Kent handed me an already opened envelope.

"You read my note?"

He shrugged as if it wasn't a big deal. "All part of the job, making sure she's not threatening to sue or something."

I stopped walking. Kent had read my note. As the manager of the course, he was privy to everything, but knowing he read Page's letter bothered me. "Next time, let me be the first to read her notes."

His eyes narrowed briefly, then he smiled again. "She is a pretty thing, isn't she?"

"You've been hanging around with my grandfather too much. There's more to a woman than looks. When you wake up and realize it's the twenty-first century, let me know."

He ignored me, pulled out his keys and unlocked his office door.

I eyed him as he pocketed the keys and stepped inside. "There it is. You're now the proud owner of a one-legged chicken."

Sure enough. A chicken sat on top of Kent's desk. It was a fat red hen that bobbed its head back and forth.

"Hey, get down off there." Kent tried to shoo it off of the desk, but the bird hopped on top of his keyboard and left a sticky present for him.

"Get off of there!" Kent cried out.

I wrinkled my nose as I watched Kent chase the chicken around the office. It might have had only one leg, but it was fast. Hopping from desk to chair to windowsill, it squawked as Kent reached for it. It hurried to his bookshelf and began hopping from shelf to shelf as though it were a ladder.

I leaned against the door frame as I watched Kent jump up and down, trying to reach for her. "If I'd known it would be this entertaining, I would have taken a video so I could enjoy it again later."

What was I getting myself into with Page? Watching Kent chase the chicken around the office had been the highlight of my week—second only to meeting Page. I only wished she'd been there to see the chicken-chase in action.

"Shut up," Kent grunted.

The chicken flew down from its perch and scurried to the corner where it hid under a chair. "You're terrifying it, Kent."

He rested his hands behind his head while he caught his breath. "It's faster than it looks. Besides, a little terror might do it some good. Teach it not to crap on my keyboard."

"You should start doing more cardio and fewer weights. That chicken's giving you quite a workout."

He muttered something back to me as I pulled Page's note out of the envelope.

It was a legitimate handwritten note on thick paper with a sketch on the front of a golfer on the green—I wondered if she drew it.

Dear Noah,

I'm so incredibly sorry about killing your <u>legendary</u> mascot. I know you must be heartbroken. I'm sending you Edwina to keep you company, and hopefully, fill Lucifer's void. Maybe she'll become a new urban legend to help you gain more members. I'll be back to make sure you're getting along.

Page Boone

She left a note—and a chicken—for me. I needed to get her phone number. She'd underlined legendary, and I could read her sarcasm coming through the note.

I left Kent to deal with the chicken situation while I went back to work in my office. It was good for him to be stretched this way.

I pulled up the marketing plan that Kent had created together. When my grandpa was running the course, it had been the boys' club. Men with money and time on their hands, getting together to talk about their money. I intended to change that. Our new plan was an all-inclusive plan. It even including targeting families. Alec Dunaway would be horrified to see a child golfing on the course. I happened to think it was an excellent way to foster a love of golf in future generations.

My grandfather expected me to fail as the owner of

this course—I expected him to watch me succeed. He'd be hyperventilating when he saw the changes we planned to incorporate—he couldn't stand children.

He would have a fit when he found out new members didn't have to be in a certain income bracket. My grandfather liked money. He liked to spend it, smell it, and talk about it, but he was never very good at keeping it. He always talked investors into lending him money for a business that he would inevitably run into the ground. Then he would leave the mess behind to someone else and blame them for his failure.

Once I finished my phone calls, I slipped on my jacket and buttoned the front, remembering the way Page had helped me put it on the other day. Such a simple action shouldn't linger that long in a man's mind, but all I could think about was her slender hands helping me into my coat. Those nimble fingers buttoning it up, then her hand patting my chest and sending my heart into overdrive. It was a little embarrassing to admit to myself how often I'd relived that moment in my mind.

I walked down the back staircase and slipped through the side door into the lobby. I checked in at the front desk with Alisha and Mandy.

"How is everything going?" I asked.

"Slow today, but we have two new member applications," Mandy answered.

"And there's a guest here," Alisha said as she waggled her eyebrows. "Maybe he'll become a member too. He's in the pro shop right now."

Mandy looked a little starry-eyed too, so I could guess that this guest was young and good looking. Kids these days—getting obsessed with someone they just met—not unlike me.

"Make sure you guys take your breaks this morning.

And let me know when you have your school schedules figured out."

"I can work anytime I'm not in class," Alisha replied. "I'll give you my class schedule."

"What about homework?"

"People do homework?" She smiled.

I exaggerated my eye roll so she would see. "You can have however many hours you want here, but I expect you to make time for homework. You're paying for college. Make it count."

Now it was her turn to roll her eyes. "I'll let you know."

"Sounds good. I'll go check in at the shop. Neither of you wants a chicken, do you?"

They both burst out laughing. "Page made us promise to not spoil the surprise by calling you. She's fun."

"She is at that. Kent's still trying to catch that thing."

"She brought it in a pet carrier. She wanted to say hi to you if you were close by," Mandy explained. "We couldn't find you, and she said she had to head to work."

"Are you dating her?" Alisha asked.

"Not yet," I smiled.

"I heard she turned Kent down flat," Mandy told me.

"Hmm, interesting." I tried to smile at that, but it troubled me that Kent had tried to ask her out—especially when I had made it clear I was interested in her. Although, it only made me like Page more knowing that she'd turned him down. Smart woman.

"Yeah, I overheard him telling a couple of the caddies about it. Said they didn't stand a chance since she admitted she's waiting for you," Mandy said with a laugh.

She *liked* me. She liked *me*. She was waiting for me. I didn't think anyone could wipe the smile off my face for the rest of the day.

Shaking my head, I walked toward the pro shop. It was

the one section of The Garden that didn't need to be reno-
vated. Grandfather had been meticulous about that part of
the golf course.

When I stepped inside the pro shop, I immediately
spotted the guest the girls had been talking about. He stood
a head above the man and woman he was with, and a
good six inches taller than the club pro—Robert, not Bob
—who was helping them. Robert nodded when he noticed
me. I waved him off to let him know he should continue
working with the trio. I walked behind the sales desk and
logged onto the computer to find out how many golfers
were out on the green.

I overheard the woman say, "Well, I don't know. Our
good luck charm is gone now."

"Mom, you're a terrible golfer. No amount of luck will
fix that."

I had to bite my cheek to keep from laughing. I stole a
discreet look over the computer monitor at the couple and
son as they debated over which grip would be better for
their golf clubs.

I did a double take when I realized it was the same
couple that Page had been golfing with the other day.

They sorted through the handgrips Robert held out for
them. I wondered how they knew Page. She hadn't wanted
to be golfing that day—that was obvious from the fact
she'd been passing notes to my staff and napping on the
green.

Curiosity got the better of me. I shut off the computer
and slipped around the counter.

"Maybe I could help you pick the right grip. You don't
mind, Robert?"

Robert looked at me like he might cry with joy. He
wasn't the most patient person with beginners. He was
obsessive about golf, and he was born with a club in his

hand. But when people came into the shop with zero previous knowledge, he had to fight himself to keep from running away. He was so knowledgeable that I gave him a raise when I took over the course and promised to sponsor him in a couple of golf tournaments. With him being well-respected in the golf community, he was a great draw for new members. Besides, he loved giving lessons to the more talented golfers on the course.

"Oh, you're the man that ran off with Page the other day!" The woman faced me with wide eyes.

I smiled stiffly. "Yes, I didn't want her to have to be around that snake any longer, or to be harassed by some— shall we say—dedicated Lucifer fans."

"Such a shame. Such a big snake snuffed out like that." The older man snapped his fingers and shook his head sadly. "Yes, I can't believe we forgot all about Page after you took her away. So many people were trying to talk to us that we forgot she rode with us. I'm afraid we left without her to avoid all the questions. Such a shame that snake was killed, though."

I straightened a little at that—as if it were her fault that the giant had struck at her. "It wasn't her fault. I should have had Lucifer moved a long time ago."

The younger man muttered something under his breath that sounded like "Amen."

I turned to him, and even though I was a solid six feet, I still had to look up. He stuck out his hand. "I'm Mack. Page is my cousin. These are my parents, Tricia and Mike."

The relief that this guy was her cousin was nearly palatable. He wasn't a boyfriend. He was a cousin. I'd never been so happy to meet someone's family before.

I shook his large hand. "Noah Dunaway."

"Thanks for looking out for Page. I saw the video—that

was one heck of a swing for her, but she probably didn't tell you she's terrified of snakes."

Tricia started to say something, but Mack cut her off. "Mom, why don't you finish picking out the grip for your club? I'm going to talk to Noah for a minute."

Mack's easygoing manner put me at ease as his parents stepped back to choose their grip. I could practically see the steam rising out of Robert's head.

Mack turned back to me. "Thanks for getting Page out of the crowd before she passed out. I saw it on that video that's posted online."

"What do you mean passed out?"

He shook his head. "She's scared to death of snakes. She and another cousin, Kylie, got caught in a cottonmouth nest when they were young. Nearly died from the bites. They've both been terrified ever since—rightfully so. You don't understand just how scary that would be for Page to face a snake that size. I'd imagine she's still having nightmares."

I rubbed a hand against my forehead. I couldn't believe I'd been so insensitive. I thought it'd be fun to tease her about it; I thought it would distract her from the situation. I didn't stop to consider that she was beyond scared; she had been terrorized. Add in a history of snake encounters, and she had a legitimate phobia. How many times could one person have a cottonmouth encounter?

"She didn't tell me about that."

"Yeah, she likes to pretend like it doesn't bother her. That's why I'm glad she reacted as fast as she did instead of freezing up."

"Me too. I've had some club members asking about her —mad that she killed the snake." I shook my head. I'd watched the whole thing through my binoculars as the caddy drove across the green. That snake had struck at her even though she'd been backing away slowly. I'd never been so glad someone had swung their club.

"People get protective of rare things. They probably didn't think of the fact that it could easily kill her since she's so sensitive to the venom now."

"Isn't everyone sensitive to venom?"

Mack shoved his hands in his jeans' pockets. "Yeah, but the doctors told Page and Kylie that they were even more sensitive to future venomous bites because of how much exposure they'd had. You don't build up immunity to it— you grow more sensitive to it."

That was news to me. I'd heard of several people being bitten by cottonmouths or copperheads around here— more so in my high school years when kids were busy doing stupid stuff. It was part of living in the south, especially if you enjoyed outdoor activities. But I hadn't ever heard of anyone getting more sensitive to it.

Mack continued talking, "And then there's the fact that Page is allergic to antivenin."

"Wait. What? What's antivenin?" I rested a hand on the shelf next to me, careful to not knock down the case of golf balls.

"It's antivenom—caused anaphylactic shock in Page. She almost didn't make it the first time because of that. I was only a freshman in high school, but I still remember the doctor's face when he came out to the waiting room and told us what happened."

"Good grief."

"Yup. Most people haven't heard of that, but I guess it's a fairly common reaction."

"No wonder she looked so pale."

"She's a sensitive soul." He sighed. "You'd think she'd be tougher."

I growled. "Tougher? She's been bitten by multiple

snakes, been attacked by one this weekend, and you think she should be tougher?"

Mack grinned at my outburst. "I thought that might be the way it is. Wait until I tell Jenny."

I didn't know what he was talking about—and I was a little nervous to ask who Jenny might be. He was almost as hard to keep up with as Page.

"You like her."

I shrugged, trying to downplay it. He smirked at me, and I nodded. "Fine, yes, I like her. She's a nice girl."

Mack snorted. "Page is not a 'nice' girl. She's a unique girl, and you'd better remember that if you want to stand a chance with her. You call her nice, and you might get a golf club to your head. She hates being called nice. She thinks it's boring."

I smiled, "Noted. So how do I find her? She left me a note and a chicken this morning."

Mack chuckled, "She would. She works at an art gallery in town. She's working there tonight."

"Thanks."

Mack shrugged. "You might not be thanking me when this is all over."

I nodded. I might have a clue what he's talking about. Page had already swept into my life and stirred things up. Keeping her in my life would only shake things up even more.

I was okay with that.

Chapter Seven

PAGE

Carlotta's, the small art gallery where I worked four nights a week, was located on the outskirts of the French quarter. We had steady walk-in traffic, but very few buyers. The owner, Lottie, kept it open more as a hobby rather than a business. I didn't even know how much money she sank into it every month, but that wasn't any of my business. She paid me regularly, and I showed up regularly — a good deal for me.

She paid cash too. Rumor had it that she moved a lot of paintings through the black market. I wouldn't be surprised. There was the small locked room in the back of the gallery that she spent a lot of time in. I'd never seen the inside. She claimed it was a regular old cleaning closet.

That had three locks on it.

And alarmed access.

I was paranoid about my cleaning supplies, too, except I only kept them in a cupboard below my sink.

Glancing at my phone, I realized it was almost nine. Since it was close to closing time, I hurried to finish arranging the minute-paintings on the wall. It was a fun display of local talent. I loved the exhibit. The paintings gave a glimpse into local life, and only local artists were featured. Lottie had started the minute painting contest a year ago. Every season she would hold another minute painting contest. Artists had exactly one minute to paint something that exhibited local life or the season we were entering.

Whereas it took me about at least a month to complete a painting, these artists could paint fairly complex scenes with only sixty seconds. We awarded the top five contestants an exhibit of their own for six months. I loved that Lottie showcased others' work in such a competitive venue as the art world.

I didn't think Lottie would be too upset if I locked the front door a little early and instead focused on setting up the last of the displays. We had to prep for our wine and art night. If I closed early, I could set everything up ahead of time.

Lottie wasn't the most organized business owner, which might be why we got along great. When she wasn't out searching for priceless art, she was busy supporting local artists and talking fashion with me.

I just hoped she remembered the wine. She supposedly had a connection with a winery in California who would ship her some of their top-tier wine. We hadn't received it yet.

Maybe it would be a boxed-wine and art day.

A creaking drew my attention to the front of the shop. The oak door swung inward slowly, and a man's silhouette filled the doorway, the streetlights bright behind him. I hurried and flipped on the front bank of lights again.

Noah.

He stepped inside and shut the door. "Your sign said you were still open. If not, I can come back another time."

I shook my head and walked closer. "No, we're open. It's been a slow night, so I was thinking about closing early. But I'm glad you're here. How can I help you? Are you looking for a piece for your office?"

He smiled, and I bit my lip to keep from grinning like a fool. His voice echoed in the empty room, "No, I'm not looking for anything yet. Besides, I know someone who paints Picasso imitations, and I'd like to see those before I buy anything else."

He'd remembered that I liked to paint. And he wanted one of my imitations for his office. I could die a happy woman at the thought.

I cleared my throat. "Would you like to look through the gallery?"

He nodded and stepped farther into the room. "I mainly came to see you, but why don't you show me the gallery while I'm here?"

He came to see me. Maybe all was forgiven for the Lucifer incident. Hopefully, Edwina was a problem solver for him.

Hoping to hide my nervousness, I turned to head to the backroom, and he followed behind. "How is everything at The Garden?"

"Interesting that you should ask…"

I stopped in front of the minute paintings, and he stepped next to me. His suit jacket hung open, and he wasn't wearing a tie. The top two buttons of his shirt were unbuttoned, and he had his hands in his pants pockets. I had an overwhelming urge to draw him. He'd be the perfect model. Strong jaw, piercing eyes, and a posture that made you think the world was his for the taking.

He raised an eyebrow at me. "Kent told me we had a visitor earlier today. I would have liked to see her myself."

I nodded and played along. "That's interesting, who was this visitor?"

"From what I've heard, it was the beautiful woman who killed my snake and brought me a one-legged chicken."

I bit my lip to keep from laughing. "So, what do you think of Edwina?"

He pulled his hands from his pockets, and I studied them. Long, lean, but they look strong. The veins stood out on the backs of his hands, and I had to cross my arms to keep from reaching out to trace them. It should be against the law for a man to show his hands if they looked like that. Maybe I could convince him to sit for me someday, and I'd sketch them.

"Who is Edwina?"

"The chicken."

He scowled, but his eyes sparkled with laughter. "That thing had a name?"

"It has a name—every animal needs a name. Didn't you read my note? Your snake even had a name. Personally, I would have gone with Beelzebub for him—Lucifer is a little overdone."

Noah shook his head and ran a hand over his face. "Why did you bring me a chicken?"

I studied my peach painted toenails that peeked out from my wedge sandals. "You were so upset over losing your snake. I knew I had to make it right. When I found Edwina, I figured she would be perfect. She's a novelty, just like your snake was. She can attract new members, but now you won't have to worry about her attacking anyone since she's not poisonous." I smiled my most winning smile, hoping that would convince him I had solved all his problems.

"Actually, she attacked Kent when he came into the office today."

"That just shows she's a good judge of character."

"What do you mean by that?"

I shook my head—not sure I should tell him about Kent hitting on me. "Keep the chicken; you can trust her."

"Page, as lovely as Edwina is, I don't want a chicken on the golf course. It crapped on Kent's keyboard and chased my chef out of the office this afternoon. It's in my car right now because I didn't know what to do with it. You killed the only mascot The Garden will ever have."

He sighed, and I couldn't resist reaching out to grab his arm.

"I really can't tell you how sorry I am." Because I wasn't sorry—it was me or the snake, and I would pick me every day.

He gazed down at me, "You don't have to keep apologizing. Really."

"You know, I was doing some reading when I got home that night, and I learned that only stressed snakes bite. They rarely bite because of the current situation they are in. They only bite if they've been under prolonged stress. So being attacked by Lucifer was not my fault. It was probably because of all the stress that had been in his life before. I mean, really, the guy should have been seeing a snake charmer to help him calm down."

Noah stared at me with a blank look in his eye. "You did the only thing you could. What should I do with the chicken?"

I shrugged. "I don't know; Aunt Tricia had a friend with a little farm. They were planning to eat that chicken, so I bought it from them. Besides, how could anyone eat a one-legged chicken? It's so heartless."

"Are you a vegetarian?"

"Nope. I like my grilled chicken as much as the next person, but I don't like to look at my food when it's still alive."

Noah shook his head and chuckled. "So, I'm stuck with Edwina?"

"You can't give back a gift. Besides, I'm sure I'll be able to find you the perfect mascot if I have enough time."

He mumbled something under his breath that I didn't quite catch; I wasn't sure I wanted to.

He gestured to the paintings in front of us. "Do you enjoy working in an art gallery?"

"It's an interesting way to pass the time, and it helps keep me inspired for my art. It can be a little dull sometimes. Tonight was boring until you got here."

He nodded. "You'd rather be out painting it yourself."

"Exactly."

He turned to face me fully, "Why don't you?"

"Why don't I what?"

"Why don't you paint full time?"

I pivoted to face him. "Have you ever heard the term 'starving artist?'"

He threw his head back and laughed. It was a nice laugh that filled the gallery. "I take it you're not making a living with your art."

I fake laughed with him. "No, no, I'm not. I work other jobs so I can afford to eat and buy painting supplies."

"Why don't you sell your Picasso paintings?"

"Do you know how many imitation artists there are out there? There's probably only about a million artists out there who do imitation paintings, and I can promise you they do a better job than I do."

I sat down on the steel bench in the center of the sparse room.

Noah sat down on the opposite end of the bench. "So,

your Picassos aren't all that great. Who cares? You enjoy painting them."

Please marry me. *Thank goodness I didn't say that out loud.* "Has anyone ever told you you're a sweetheart?"

I could almost swear I saw him blush, but he ducked his head so I couldn't see.

"Well, I'd better let you get back to closing the gallery. Are you parked out back?"

"No, I'm parked a few streets over. I don't start work here until four, so by then, the streets are full."

He shoved his hands in his pockets again. "I'll wait and walk you to your car. You shouldn't be walking out alone."

"I'm used to doing things alone—it's okay."

He just smiled and shook his head. I'd have to see what I could do to keep him.

"Let me lock the back door first." I hurried around the gallery, locking windows and shutting off lights before I set the alarm and headed to the front. I grabbed Noah's hand as I walked past him and pulled him along. Once we were outside on the front sidewalk, I locked the big oak door.

"All set."

My fingers were still laced through his when I caught his amused smile. He said, "You're still holding my hand."

"It's a nice hand. Do you want me to let go?"

He shook his head and rubbed the backs of my fingers with his thumb. "You have a nice hand too."

Now he was going to make me blush. I started swinging our hands to match our stride. "So why the golf course? You're not stuffy enough to be a golf course owner. I mean, you're a little stuffy, but not too bad."

His hand squeezed mine gently. "Page, has anyone told you that you're incredibly blunt?"

"I prefer to call it pragmatic honesty. Blunt sounds so rude."

"Pragmatic honesty. All right. I could believe that." His thumb moved up to rub tiny circles on the back of my hand. I wondered how many times we could go around the block before he realized I was prolonging the walk to my car.

"So, golf course?" I reminded.

"I inherited the golf course. I didn't want it—but now I've got it, and I plan on getting it back in shape before I have a manager run it for me."

"You seemed a little stressed the other day. At first, I thought it was because of me."

"Part of it was because of you."

"I really am sorry—"

"No, you shouldn't have to be sorry," he said firmly. "We should have had that snake relocated a long time ago. He was becoming an urban legend because he was getting too comfortable with people. When I saw him strike out you, I almost lost my mind. He's a big snake. I thought he'd kill you."

"Me too. Wait—so you weren't mad at me at all? You were worried about me?"

He turned his head slightly and smiled at me. "I didn't think you'd want to be coddled right after that. But you were turning as white as a ghost, so I thought it would be better to direct your attention to something else."

"Something else! I thought you were mad at me." I stopped in the middle of the sidewalk, forcing Noah to stop as well since our hands were laced together. "You're making me mad right now!"

"You seem a little mad…"

I poked a finger at myself before I started pointing it at him. "I don't get mad, and I don't need to be 'coddled.' I definitely don't need distracted!"

Noah stood there, quietly nodding with a placid look

on his face as he watched my finger that repeatedly poke his chest. I stopped—patted his chest and smoothed his shirt. "Okay, I'm sorry. Yes, fine. I do overreact sometimes."

He chuckled. "That's all right. I don't mind."

I patted his firm chest once more, then turned and walked down the sidewalk again, pulling him with me. "You pretended to be mad about the snake so I wouldn't freak out?"

"Pretty much."

"So, I didn't destroy the golf course by getting rid of the snake?"

"No." He squeezed my hand gently.

"Thank goodness. Business should start taking off then."

"Well, we will be down on business for a while—"

What did he mean they would be down on business? Maybe Lucifer really was drawing in people. The restaurant had been full for the snake eulogy…

I didn't pay attention to the rest of what he was saying. I needed to figure out a way to help him. His livelihood was riding on a struggling golf course. I'd seen the guest book firsthand. He needed more members. Glancing up, I realized I couldn't stall the walk to my car any longer. "Oh, this is my car. Thank you for walking me."

"You're welcome." His crooked smile made me want to lean up and kiss his jaw. He'd been protective of me since the moment we met. Getting me away from the crazy snake lovers. Giving me ice water. Distracting me. Making sure I got home safely. Walking me to my car. It had been a while since someone had looked out for me in that way. I had to hurry and get out of there before I couldn't refrain from kissing him anymore.

"Well, then." I unlocked the car, climbed in, and

started it. I rolled down the window. "Don't worry—I'll come up with something to help you draw in some new business!"

His eyes widened, and he started to say something, but I was already pulling away. That man didn't want me to feel guilty. What a sweetheart! He'd been worried about *me*, not his business.

So, the chicken idea should be scratched, but I knew I would come up with something to help him draw business to the golf course. It couldn't be that hard, could it?

Chapter Eight
NOAH

Getting ready for work Friday morning, I was so busy reminiscing about my time with Page that I poured orange juice in my oatmeal bowl. I'd taken a bite before I'd realized what I'd done.

It didn't taste that good.

I remembered the soft feel of Page's hand in mine as we walked the street to her car. I'd never known hand-holding could be so much fun. I was glad when she grabbed my hand. It was exactly what I wanted to do, too, but I didn't want to come across as pushy, especially since I'd shown up to her place of work unannounced. The connection between us was tangible.

After dumping out my oatmeal, I made myself another bowl. That time, I managed to spill the milk down the front of my suit jacket. With a frustrated groan, I slipped it off and hung it up so I could take it to the dry cleaners later. I searched through my closet and found another jacket that would complement my khaki slacks. It was the jacket I'd worn the day I met Page—which only caused me to think about her more.

Thirty minutes later, after a quick shave, I promised myself I wouldn't let my thoughts of Page distract me from work that day.

I'd never been so late to a job before, and when I finally pulled into the golf course parking lot, I was determined to make some serious headway on my projects.

That is, until I walked straight into a sour smell in the hallway outside my office. I considered filing for bankruptcy right then.

Kent stood there, pretending like nothing was wrong, acting as though there wasn't a putrid smell filling the hall.

"What is that horrible smell? Is the sewer backed up?"

"Well, ah, you see, sir, ah, you see-" he coughed.

I liked Kent. He was reliable, proficient, and had many other questionable qualities. He was not—in my personal experience with him—a stutterer.

Something had to be horribly wrong. Maybe the air conditioner had stopped working and now we would have to shut down the clubhouse for a few weeks. That could be disastrous.

Closing the clubhouse would not look good and might get mentioned in the local paper. I believed there was such a thing as bad press, and I didn't want any of it.

"I didn't want to put it there, but I couldn't leave it loose, so I told her to put it in your office."

I glanced sharply at Kent. "Put what in my office? And who?"

"You know, the girl."

"There's a girl in my office."

He shook his head with impatience. "No, *she* put it in your office. I can't even say her name right now."

Page—it had to be. No one else would drop something off in my office. I remembered her parting words three nights ago. My, she had been up early to have already been here and dropped something off. Sure, I was late, but not that late.

I reached for the doorknob just as something bleated on the other side of the door. "Oh no, not that."

"I'm sorry Noah, we tried to stop her but-"

I held up my hand to stop him. "No need to explain. I understand. She's a tornado."

He nodded. "Best description I've heard all week."

My hand rested on the doorknob while I tried to decide what to do with the bleater on the other side. It was either a sheep, a goat, or a small calf. None of which should be in my office.

I opened the door and came face to face with a small goat standing on my desk. It had horns with tennis balls on the ends, and it had a piece of paper in its mouth.

Priority one: throttle Page—after I kiss her.

The goat stepped on my laptop and licked its nose.

Maybe I'd throttle her first, then kiss her.

"I'm so sorry, Noah, I told her no. She wouldn't listen." Kent complained. "She's a menace."

"You are the manager of this golf course. You could have stopped her. This is ridiculous; there's a goat on my desk!"

Kent rubbed the back of his neck. "I can't believe I'm defending the terror, but she thinks she's doing you a favor. You're the one who pretended to be upset about Lucifer."

I waved a hand at the goat, trying to get it off my desk. I regretted telling him about that.

MAA.

"I don't think it likes me." I reached towards it, planning on lifting it off my desk. Why were these animals obsessed with standing on our desks?

"Don't do it, Noah. He looks angry."

I half-turned to look at Kent again. "What's it going to do? It can't weigh over thirty pounds."

Just then, the goat bounded onto a chair then took a flying leap and slammed his hard head into my side. He sent me staggering into Kent, and we stumbled back against the wall.

The goat charged straight for my knees; I barely had time to dodge its horns.

"Quick!" I yelled. "You grab one side, and I'll grab the other."

We each grabbed a horn and a back leg.

"Now what?" Kent asked as he struggled to hold the kicking leg.

"Now we find old McDonald and return this thing to its farm. Did she say where it came from?"

"I was too surprised to ask," Kent admitted.

I groaned and tried my best to stretch my side without releasing my hold on the horn. The ornery goat had definitely bruised my ribs.

"Ouch!" Kent yelled. The little goat bit his leg when he leaned too close.

"Let's go find an empty closet where we can stash this thing until we figure out what to do with it."

"All we have are supply closets. It'd probably eat everything in them."

"What about a bathroom stall? The downstairs women's bathroom has the floor to ceiling doors," I suggested.

"Perfect. Let's go. And then how about you go clear things up with Page before she sends a tiger next?"

Kent was right. This wasn't wholly Page's fault. I must not have made it very clear last night when I told her she shouldn't feel any guilt about the whole ordeal. She was trying to help, and while I appreciated the sentiment it was still horrible. The last thing I needed right now was a bunch of animals running around the golf course.

We carried the tyrannical goat downstairs and into the women's bathroom. We closed the toilet lid and then slapped a "closed for maintenance" sign on the stall door.

"There, that should take care of that for a little while. I'll call my sister; she lives in the country. Maybe the kids want a pet goat."

Kent nodded. "Please do. While you're at it, get rid of Page."

I chuckled, "I thought you said she was hilarious and refreshing."

He shook his head. "No, I think my exact words were she's annoying and interfering."

"You're just mad because the chicken crapped on your Armani watch when you carried it outside."

He glared at me. "You better believe I'm mad about that. She owes me a new watch."

"You're the one who stuck the one-legged chicken in your office."

"Excuse me?" A woman interrupted us as we stood in the center of the women's restroom arguing. She leaned around the doorway, looking at us expectantly.

I straightened my jacket. "No, excuse us, we were just looking into a—um—maintenance issue."

Kent nodded politely to the woman, and we hurried out of the bathroom.

"All right, I need to go talk to my new servers that are supposed to be here at eleven. You go find some food and water for that thing. Hopefully, Dani will want the goat. She took the chicken—what's one more animal?"

"Why do I have to feed it?"

"Because you're overpaid and need to earn your keep." I grinned as Kent glared at me.

"Fine. I'll feed the devil goat as long as you take care of the Page situation tonight. No more animals. None. No snakes, no chickens, no goats. I don't want another deadly or pooping thing on this golf course."

He'd make a wonderful manager. I mock saluted him and turned on my heel. Honestly, I hoped I could leave the golf course in Kent's hands soon. He took pride in it and invested in the business.

When I first started at the golf course, I'd been wary of my grandfather's most recent hire: Kent. Turned out that it was one of the best things my grandfather had done for the course. Kent had a mind for business, was surprisingly good at people, and adored golf. All of those reasons were why we'd worked out the details of him buying into the business and becoming part owner. But we had too much to do for me to hand it over to him just yet.

Hopefully, the new chef and revamped menu would give us the jumpstart we needed. Tonight, I'd talked with Page and convince her that the animals weren't necessary. All without hurting her feelings, then I would try to persuade her to go on a date with me. I didn't have time to date, but I would *make* time for Page. Something told me I would regret it for the rest of my life if I didn't try.

I headed upstairs, smelling distinctly like a billy goat. One thought on my mind—to explain to Page that I wasn't mad at her—well maybe for the goat incident—and that she could stop sending strange animals. The golf course didn't need a circus; it needed a facelift and a new menu.

At six o'clock, I stepped into the front lobby of The Garden. Interviewing the potential staff had gone well, and I hired three of them on for a two-week trial basis. Over the lunch hour, I ran home and showered so I wouldn't smell like a goat anymore. Then I headed back to my office and set up an appointment with the chef my friend had recommended.

When I stepped inside the lobby, the number of voices overwhelmed me. It was a madhouse in there. I'd never seen so many people waiting to play golf.

At least two hundred people filled the lobby. Unfortunately, our lobby's fire code only allowed one hundred twenty. I didn't even know if we were equipped to handle that many people at the same time. I knew for a fact we didn't have that much rental equipment if they all planned on golfing.

It would be absolute mayhem. I pushed my way through the crowd so that I could help at the front desk.

I had to squeeze between a group of friends, greet several women who introduced themselves, and finally arrived at the front desk in a rumpled state.

"Look, there he is." It was an echo of the same words rippling across the crowd.

A woman stepped in front of me just before I could

walk around the desk. "My name is Tammy, and I can't tell you how excited I am to meet you."

She extended her hand and her chest about the same distance. I took a step backward and reached out to shake her hand. "Welcome to The Garden. I hope you enjoy your time here."

I slipped around her and hurried to the desk. Mandy and Alisha were rapidly taking people's names and registering them. "What is going on?"

"It's been like this for the last half-hour," Alisha told me. "They've been asking when you would come down. I told them that sometimes you visit with guests, but sometimes you're busy with other things. They've been insane."

"Is there a problem they want to talk to me about?"

"Mr. Dunaway. I don't think they're here to play golf," Mandy popped up.

"What do you mean?"

"Look out there." She pointed at the sea of people. That was when I noticed something unusual.

It was all women.

Women everywhere. Young, old, middle-aged. They were all here.

Now, I have nothing against women. I love them. But this crowd was not dressed for a game of golf. Stiletto heels and short dresses. Cream-colored sandals and floor-length dresses. "What. Are. They. Doing?"

Four of the women crowded closer to the front desk, and it forced the three of us to break apart from our little huddle.

I put on my best customer service smile even though I was confused as heck. "Hello, how can I help you today?"

They smiled simultaneously; it reminded me of synchronized swimming.

"We're so excited about singles night. It's such a

wonderful idea. And when we saw your picture, we just knew we had to sign up," one young brunette gushed. She looked close to Page's age, but there was something crazy in her eyes that made me want to run away.

I took a step back, afraid that the top of her shirt might give out, and something might escape. "I'm afraid I'm a little confused."

She slid a piece of paper across the desk. "It was all over social media the last few days."

I waited until she moved her hand before I picked it up to read.

Singles Mingle at The Garden.

Meet an eligible bachelor, enjoy a romantic evening on a magical golf course, and experience the romance and warm southern nights in a way you never have before.

Underneath, it had my picture, the golf course hours, and the address.

Admittedly, it was a great photo. It was the one I use on my social media and website photo. It was professionally done and the closest I would ever get to looking like a male model. Except these women didn't seem to notice the difference between me and the photo. Maybe they couldn't smell the desperation rolling off of me. The fact that these women could become members at the course or spend money at the restaurant made me want to keep them somehow.

"Ladies!" I called. "Ladies, if I could have your attention for a moment. There seems to be a misunderstanding. I was not aware of any singles night tonight. Apparently, I need to fire my social media manager."

I forced a chuckle; only a few of them laughed with me. "While this isn't singles mingle night, we are testing out a brand-new menu in the club restaurant, and we would love to have you join us and hear your feedback on the menu. We are running our happy hour specials right now. Thank you for your time and for coming out at such late notice."

There was an audible sigh that swept across the room.

I slipped around the edge of the desk. "If you all would follow me, I'll lead you to the restaurant."

The brunette came to stand much too close to me. "What a funny misunderstanding!"

Her laugh echoed loudly over the steady hum of the other voices.

It was the first time I'd escorted a hundred women to dinner. The restaurant was relatively empty—not uncommon these days. Layton hurried and opened the banquet room as well and seated a third of the women there.

"So, how did you become the single bachelor for tonight?"

I jumped at the close voice. I glanced down at the same brunette who was now standing plastered to my arm.

"You must not have heard, but there was a misunderstanding."

"What a shame," she said as she made a pouty face.

"Yes, isn't it?" I took a step back, and she followed.

"My name is Gabbie."

Clearing my throat, I looked around for Kent. He was standing in the center of the room, laughing with a group of women. He was never nearby when I needed him. "I hope you have a wonderful evening, Gabbie."

Her hand latched onto my forearm, and I got a chill. It

wasn't even remotely close to the electric current I experienced with Page.

"Don't be a stranger," she ended her words in a whisper as she leaned closer.

I snatched my arm away.

"I need to go mingle now," I said with a grimace as she leaned closer still.

Mingle? More like get away from her…

The rest of the night, I mingled. I became the model *mingler*. They came out expecting to meet other single people, and since most of the women stayed and became paying customers, it was the least I could do. I was surprised to enjoy myself, and had several interesting conversations, including getting to explain the benefits of taking up golf as a hobby.

I was given approximately fifty cellphone numbers "In case I changed my mind."

Unfortunately, I still didn't have the one number that I wanted — Page's. But I knew where she worked, and I intended to pay her another visit soon. She was creating too much notoriety around the golf course and it had to stop. I could practically see her fingerprints all over this single's mingle night.

If I made it out of the night alive, I'd put a stop to it.

"Wow, I didn't know this was a women only event."

I turned around to find Hagen Raglund standing at the entrance of the restaurant. His messy hair and ripped jeans made him look like he just stepped in from boys' night out. No man had ever looked so good to me. I nearly cried with relief.

"Noah Dunaway, what are you doing here?"

"Hagen, I can honestly say I'm thrilled to see you."

"That's something new." He grinned.

Hagen and I grew up alongside each other—not necessarily together. Our parents always forced us to the same social events growing up. I'd spent a lot of my growing up years with Hagen's older brother, Branton, who was my age. Hagen always managed to make a nuisance of himself. We didn't hate each other, but usually we didn't love to see each other, and I didn't feel chummy in the slightest.

Tonight, I'd make an exception.

"What excellent timing. If I remember right, you broke up with your girlfriend—and are now single and available." I stepped closer to him as I gestured to the crowd in front of us. "Want to mix and mingle?"

He stepped back and held up a hand to wave me off. "I'm engaged. But my friend Dave here is single and ready to mingle."

He nodded to the middle-aged, balding man with him who had yet to pull his attention away from the room full of women.

"Noah, this is my neighbor Dave."

"Hi," Dave said quietly, still not looking my way. It was pointless to try and get his attention.

"You're engaged to Brooke?" I'd never liked Hagen's ex-girlfriend. She was a little too mercenary for me. I liked the idea of having some type of emotion in my relationships. It had always surprised me that Hagen had stayed with her for longer than a week.

Hagen shook his head. "Nope. I found a nice girl who likes to keep me on my toes."

"That's good to hear," I told him, and sincerely meant it.

Hagen cleared his throat. "So, I'm happily engaged, and you're here mingling at a singles dinner."

"It's even worse than that. I'm running this golf course. These women thought we were hosting a singles dinner."

Hagen chuckled. "I'd say I felt sorry for you, but this is too funny. We just came in from playing. A caddy told us your main attraction is dead."

I looked at him sharply. "Not you too. Snake follower?"

He jerked his thumb over his shoulder at Dave, who was now chatting with a woman somewhere in his same age vicinity.

"I promised Dave I'd go golfing with him. He told me about The Garden and how it had a record-breaking snake."

"It's still hard to believe people came here to see it. How ridiculous can they be?"

Hagen shrugged. "I hear you. But tell me what're you doing with a golf course?"

"Grandpa left this to me—a parting shot. Wants to watch me fail."

"Aha. That sounds like the old Dunaway we all know and dislike. What are you going to do about it?"

I pulled my phone out of my pocket and glanced at the time. "Well, it seems as though I've inherited a fairy godmother."

"How so?"

"The woman who killed the snake. She's trying to help me with the golf course. Trying to help me market." I gestured towards the room. "This is her doing."

Hagen's eyes sharpened on me. "What did you say her name was?"

"I didn't. But it's Page Boone."

"Page Boone? You sure?" Hagen asked as he stood up straight again.

"Yes, I'm sure."

Hagen laughed incredulously.

"She's…fun. She's made running a golf course a lot more interesting than I thought it would be."

Hagen smiled, and he looked positively maniacal. "So, you're dating this girl?"

"No, not yet."

He laughed. "Good luck. You'll need it."

I flexed my shoulders. "You know her?"

"Pretty sure. There can't be too many Page Boone's in the area. I'm marrying her cousin. I hadn't realized she was the snake killer—I'm not surprised, though. Kylie was whispering about something with her the other night."

Maybe I should attempt to be Hagen's friend, for once. I could go golf a few rounds with him and learn a few things about Page…but then I noticed his evil smirk and decided against it. "How many cousins does she have? I've already met one."

"About fifty. I'm still not sure." Hagen shrugged as if it wasn't a big deal.

I didn't think I had that many people in my entire family tree. "How well do you know Page?"

"She threatened me with a baseball bat when I picked up Kylie for our first date, so I guess you could say we're friends."

"Probably a good thing you didn't make her use that bat. She's got a fantastic swing. You should see her with a golf club."

Hagen leaned against the doorframe and glanced around the crowd. He frowned when his eyes landed on Gabbie. Her eyes locked on us, and she wiggled her fingers in a little wave.

"Page set this up tonight?"

"I'm nearly positive," I answered. "She feels bad that she killed our mascot. She's sent me a one-legged chicken and a goat."

Hagen laughed loudly enough to turn heads our way—

at least the few that weren't already staring. "She must really like you."

"Why do you say that?"

"She'd ignore you if she wasn't interested."

I smiled. I needed to thank her for the violent goat then strangle her for the singles mingle night "I guess I'll have to go visit her at work tonight."

"Page is hanging out with her brother tonight. Kylie's was over there having dinner with them while I was golfing."

"Think I could get her number from you?"

"Nah. That's too personal," he answered, shaking his head with a frown. "But I'll text you the address."

"As if that's better," I muttered. I could have asked Kent for that, but I didn't really want to tell him where I was going. He'd seemed upset at the mention of Page's name ever since the goat incident earlier that morning.

Hagen shrugged. "I'm going to get Dave out of here before he plans a weekend trip to Vegas. Tell Page I said hi."

Hagen's evil chuckle floated my way as he walked out with Dave.

Hagen knew my Page. I wasn't sure how I felt about that. We'd competed for so much over the years I didn't think I liked the idea that he knew the girl I was interested in. Then again, he was already engaged to her cousin. Maybe that would keep him out of the way.

But right then, all I wanted to do was go see Page and not worry about Hagen. No more single ladies' nights, and no more goats.

I smiled as I walked to my office to grab my car keys. My phone lit up with a text from Hagen telling me the address.

Time to go get a girl.

Chapter Nine

PAGE

The doorbell rang as I washed the last of the dinner dishes. Mom and Dad were out on their date night, so I was hanging out with my little brother Cameron at their house.

The clock on the wall said eight. Eight at night seemed too late for a package to be delivered. We weren't expecting anyone else to stop by. Kylie was the only one we'd planned on, and she had already left. People did not stop by my mother's house unannounced. It simply wasn't done.

Glancing down the hall, I made sure Cameron was still at the back of the house. Next, I grabbed the baseball bat that Dad kept in the entryway closet and peeked through the peephole.

Noah Dunaway stood outside the door.

He was quite possibly the only man who looked that good through a peephole. He even looked great with a giant head. My heart sped up as I unlocked the door and opened it.

I tried for a casual pose by leaning on the baseball bat

with one hand, but the bat slipped against Mom's polished wood floor, and my face slammed into the door frame.

"Whoa, you okay?" Noah's hand latched onto my arm as he pulled me upright. The warmth of his hand sent tingles up my arm.

"Oh, I'm great. Fine. What are you doing here? Did you get my present? Isn't it perfect? Everyone loves goats. Just look at how goat yoga took off. Isn't he adorable?"

He raised an eyebrow at me and said in a rye voice, "You and I must be talking about two different goats."

"What did Zeke do?" I swung the door wide and motioned for Noah to come in.

"Zeke?" he asked as he stepped inside and looked around.

"Yes. Ezekiel. The goat."

"Ah, yes, Zeke is happily at my sister's little farm now, but not before he broke the keyboard on my laptop, ate a couple of invoices in my office, and chewed the door handle off the bathroom stall."

I covered my mouth with my hand. "Why was he in the bathroom?"

"We didn't know what else to do with him. Kent left him in there until my sister picked him up."

I shook my head. It was so hard to find good employees these days. If people couldn't even figure out where to put a goat, were they any help running a golf course? I didn't think so.

"Come in; we're about to make some popcorn and watch a movie. Tell me all about it."

To my surprise, he nodded, slipped off his shoes like a civilized person should, and followed me to the kitchen. Finally, a man who didn't bring disgusting, germy shoes into the house.

I glanced down as he walked beside me. His thin, black

dress socks made my fuzzy purple socks stand out even brighter. When we reached the kitchen, he leaned against the counter while I popped a bag of popcorn in the microwave. He folded his arms across his chest and crossed his ankles. He filled the kitchen. I could feel his presence everywhere.

It was too much, but I loved it. I didn't know why he was standing in my parents' house, but I wouldn't argue with whatever brought him. His eyes were on me as I dumped the popcorn in the bowl. I didn't know if men like him ate popcorn, but women like me do. Shoving a handful of popcorn in my mouth, I called Cameron.

"Popcorn's done!"

Cameron dashed into the room.

"Hmm, thanks Page," he said as he shoveled a couple of handfuls popcorn in his mouth. He finished chewing before he realized there was a stranger in our kitchen. So strange that he wasn't aware of Noah's presence from the minute he knocked on our door the way I was.

"Cameron, this is Noah. Noah, this is my little brother, Cameron."

Noah smiled and shook Cameron's hand. I could count on one hand how many times I'd seen Cameron blush, but this was one of them. He straightened his small shoulders and gripped Noah's large hand with his thin ten-year-old hand. "Nice to meet you."

I nodded approvingly. Mom and Dad were teaching the cretin some manners. I'd have to tell them what a good job they were doing.

"I'm stuck with Page on Mom and Dad's date nights, even though I'm old enough to stay home by myself. Page says I'll never be old enough to stay home by myself." He rolled his eyes, and I reached over to pinch his side.

"Better me than the twins," I reminded him.

He shuddered then told Noah while rolling his eyes again, "Lilly and Laney are so annoying."

Noah glanced at me with an amused smile on his face.

"They're seventeen," I explained.

"Aha. I remember when my sister was seventeen. She was so annoying too." He winked at Cameron, and I nearly melted on the spot.

"Are you staying to watch a movie with us?" Cameron asked.

Noah glanced at me, but I tried to keep a stoic face. I didn't know what Noah wanted with me. I knew what I wanted from him, but also knew I was a faster mover than most. If I decided I wanted something, I went for it and thought about the consequences later.

"I just stopped by to talk to your sister for a few minutes."

"Are you sure you want to miss out on Indiana Jones?" Cameron waggled his eyebrows at Noah, and Noah laughed.

He had a nice laugh. I sighed, and he glanced my way. Oops. I grabbed a handful of popcorn and shoveled it into my mouth.

Noah smiled knowingly at me before he turned back to Cameron. "I could never turn down Indiana Jones." He picked up the bowl of popcorn. "Lead the way."

Cameron jumped up and down excitedly as the three of us headed to the living room.

"Which one are we watching?" Noah asked.

"Not the fourth one," Cameron and I said simultaneously.

After a few rounds of *eenie-meenie-minie-mo*, we settled on the first one.

Noah sat down in the middle of the couch, holding the

bowl of popcorn. Cameron leaped onto the sofa next to him, no qualms about pressing up against a stranger's side.

We were a little too alike. I'd have to keep a closer eye on him.

Noah glanced up at me and patted the seat next to him. I smiled and sat down, tucking my feet under me. He tilted the bowl of popcorn towards me and smiled.

I could never tire of that sight—popcorn and a smile.

The movie didn't hold my attention since I'd probably seen it twenty times before. All I could think about was a somewhat stoic golf course owner who was sitting on my couch in a suit and tie, eating popcorn. He was careful not to crowd my space on the couch, but it was impossible to ignore the heat or the smell of cinnamon gum wafting from him.

It was my new favorite scent.

Our hands brushed each time we reached into the bowl.

Cameron fell asleep halfway through the movie, and Noah carried him to bed for me. I didn't want to leave him on the couch. Once he fell asleep, he was dead to the world, poor guy. As pesky as he was, I loved him to pieces. I think there was a big enough age gap between us that I felt protective of him rather than annoyed. He was a sweet kid, and I'm pretty sure I'd do anything for him. That's why I didn't mind hanging out on date nights with him. Soon he would be way too cool to hang out with his big sister. I intended to soak this up while it lasted. Maybe when I was old and feeble, he'd come to visit me in the nursing home.

"Thank you for helping me get him in bed. He's not as easy to carry as when he was five."

Noah smiled and followed me into the kitchen again.

The movie still played in the background. "He seems like a good kid."

"He is." I took a sip of my iced tea. Caffeine was always a good idea. "So. You just stopped by tonight for movie night?"

He took the tea I offered him, then set it down on the counter. "I have a confession to make."

Uh oh. Nothing good ever came after words like that. What kind of confession? He routinely stole cinnamon gum? Did he wear tennis shoes without socks? The options were endless.

"I don't want a mascot for the golf course. No animals. Really, the course isn't doing too bad. If you're worried about me, don't be."

I'd known it was a bad idea, but he'd seemed so upset about his lack of mascot that I didn't want to let him down. "I thought that's what you were looking for—a way to draw in business."

"I don't want a mascot," he repeated.

"You don't?"

I leaned against the counter and rested my head on my hands as I stared at him.

He explained about Lucifer, "My grandpa, who left the golf course to me, had that snake imported from the bayou."

"What? What kind of crazy person does that?

"My grandpa. By the way, I met your cousin today."

I coughed, trying to hide the panic. "Oh, no—which one?"

"I met Mack."

"Aha." I sighed with relief. Mack was one of the best cousins he could have met. He was kind to everyone. Jenny would have been a loose cannon. She made me look like a diplomat compared to her level of tact.

"He told me about when you were a kid. At first, I thought he was going to tear my head off for letting the snake get that close to you. He explained about your allergy. No wonder you were terrified."

I stared at the counter, a little embarrassed that Mack had told him everything. "Mack's such a sweetheart. He refuses to take me out on any hikes with him because he's worried I'll get bit again."

Noah chuckled, "Why do I get the impression you still go on hikes?"

I traced an imaginary pattern on the counter with my index finger. "I do. You're sworn to secrecy though, because Mack would have a heart attack."

"Let's make a deal." Noah leaned forward and rested his arms on the counter.

"What kind of deal are we talking about?"

"Next time you feel the need to go for a hike, you take me."

I bit my lip to keep from grinning. "Are you sure your legs are up for it? All that sitting behind a desk, you might not be up to the task."

He smirked. "Isn't that an even better reason to go hiking?"

"Excellent point. We've got to keep you healthy." I smiled as I stared at his chest. Noah didn't need any help to stay fit. It was obvious he didn't spend all his time behind a desk. "You know, I hear that Zeke likes to go on regular walks. You could take him out with you—to help you fight off obesity."

"I think I had enough exercise today."

"Oh?"

"The goat wasn't the only running I did today. There were exactly one hundred and twenty-two women who came into the club today thinking we were having auditions for a local Bachelor show. They thought I was the bachelor."

I took a big drink of my tea and promptly choked.

He narrowed his eyes at me. "You wouldn't know anything about this, would you?"

I shook my head as I kept coughing. Finally, when I could speak again, I asked, "Did it help widen your demographic?"

"I now have twenty new members, and I've already had to hide around corners to avoid them—in only one evening. I'll have to think of a way to become attached to someone. If I had a girlfriend, I could tell them that."

I forced myself not to raise my hand as a volunteer to make him unavailable.

It wasn't hard to garner attention for it. Posting his profile picture on a few strategic local social media groups, he started getting likes and comments. I thought it'd be a good way to diversify his clients. There might have been some assumptions that people made... that I didn't bother correcting.

One thing was for sure: it bothered me to think of other women chasing after him even though I was the one who sent them. Maybe I hadn't thought that part through when I'd planned a single ladies' night.

"Well, how are we going to solve this problem?"

He stood up and carried his cup to the sink, "I'm open to suggestions."

"Hmm, well, you could go through with it. Host your own version of The Bachelor."

He muttered under his breath as he turned around to face me. He shoved his hands in his pockets and stepped closer to me. "I'm not going to date a bunch of strange women just to save my golf course."

"That's not very self-sacrificial."

"I'm not that kind of guy."

"What a shame." I opened the Tupperware lid to the chocolate chip cookies Kylie had baked for my parents when she was over earlier. Smelling the delicious aroma, I broke a small bite off and ate it.

"What are you going to do about it?" His voice was so low it was almost a whisper.

"What am I going to do about it? It's not my golf course." I took another step closer.

"You sent the women," he reminded me with a pointed look.

Technically, I didn't. They sent themselves. But he didn't look like he was in the mood to argue. I tried my best for an apologetic, innocent expression. "I just wanted to help you."

The corner of his mouth twitched up. "I appreciate that, but next time, why don't you come into the office and talk with me about it? Or better yet, you can give me your phone number, and I'll call you with a mayday whenever single women hunt me up at the golf course."

He held his hand out expectantly.

I slapped a cookie in it. He raised both eyebrows. "Your phone."

"Oh." I pulled my phone from my pocket and unlocked it before I handed it to him. He typed something on it and then I heard a chime. I could only assume he'd sent himself a text. He reached past me and set the phone down on the counter, crowding my space but careful not to touch me. I didn't want to breathe.

He leaned back and shoved his hands in his pockets, again. "I better get going, it's getting late. But I'm looking forward to you helping me with my single-lady problem."

"Don't worry. I'll take care of it. As long as I can sing some Beyoncé," I promised with a smile.

"We'll talk soon." He walked out of the kitchen and to the front door. When he grabbed the handle, he turned to look at me. He looked surprised to find me standing behind him, but my mom always taught me it was rude not to walk a guest to the door.

"Page Boone."

"Yes?"

"You're something else. Don't change."

With that, he left me standing there with a bad case of butterflies in my stomach and stars in my eyes.

Stopping in front of the pet store on the way to work the next morning, I snapped a picture of the sign, then texted it to Noah. Pete's Pets.

Next, I snapped a picture of a fluffy white puppy to him.

Page: Trying to find you that perfect little something.

His response was immediate.

. . .

Noah: Not that. Anything but that.

Page: You don't mean that. Everybody needs a pet.

Noah: If you want to do something nice for me, why don't you have dinner with me?

Page: Only if we have Beignets for dinner.

Noah: Sweet tooth?

Page: Sweet *teeth* and lover of fried things.

Noah: If I promise to give you beignets, will you promise to NOT buy me a dog?

Page: It's a deal.

I shoved my phone into my small clutch then opened the door to the pet store. I'd promised him I wouldn't buy him a dog. That didn't mean I couldn't find something else for him.

Chapter Ten

NOAH

I left the all-staff meeting feeling more discouraged than I had in a while. Half my kitchen staff was threatening to quit because my new head chef demanded perfection. Reggie promised to stay on only if he got along with the new head chef, but we all knew he only seemed to know how to make greasy foods you would find at an average diner.

It was a relief to end the meeting, and now I could go back to my office and focus on deciding the future menu of the restaurant. Xavier had sent me someone he highly recommended, and I hoped it would give me the edge I needed. Xavier had found me a chef who had recently moved from the Los Angeles area. Mason Walsh. After reading his credentials and knowing I could trust Xavier's recommendation, I hired the new chef on the spot.

"Are you sure letting half of the kitchen staff quit is the best idea?" Kent asked as he followed me into my office.

"Yes, I think it's time we got fresh faces. The new hires are starting today, so that will be good. If the old staff isn't happy—"

A knock on the office door interrupted me, and we turned to stare at the door.

"Yes?"

"Excuse me, sir? We have a delivery for you."

"Come in," I answered. The large oak door swung inward, revealing Alisha from the front desk, and a man with gray hair and leathery skin, wearing a green uniform standing behind her. He held a large box with holes in it and the sides. One hand held the strings to several colorful balloons.

"Which one of you am I supposed to sing to?" he asked.

"That depends on who it's from," Kent told him.

"This is from a Page Boone."

"Oh, no. Not again. I thought you had taken care of that," Kent groaned.

"I thought I had, too," I replied. "I guess I'll have to call her."

"And I thought my girlfriends were high maintenance."

"How could your girlfriends possibly be high maintenance? You only date them for a week."

"Which one of you is Noah? I'm supposed to sing before I deliver." The delivery man took a step forward, impatient to be on his way.

"Let's do us all a favor," I suggested. "And we'll call it even if I take that box from you—without the singing."

"Good enough for me." The man looked relieved.

"Alisha, you can go back down to reception. Sir, you can just set that box here on the desk."

"What about the balloons?" The deliveryman asked.

"Better hand those to Kent."

"Thanks for nothing," Kent complained.

The deliveryman left the room. Kent and I stared at the box containing who knew what from Page Boone. I didn't know how she kept surprising me, but a singing delivery did the trick.

"Who wants to open it?"

"It's addressed to you, boss."

"Stop calling me boss. You run this golf course as much as I do. Fine, I'll open it." I swallowed the lump in my throat and pried open the top of the wooden box. I was pleasantly surprised that nothing jumped out and bit me. It was a small tank with two geckos in it. There was a note taped to the tank. I carefully lifted the box out and set the geckos—and their home—on my desk, then pulled the envelope off and ripped it open:

Dear Noah,

I'm sorry for sending you Zeke and Edwina, but I hope they've brought some adventure to your so, so, so boring life. I know that deep down, you want a mascot there ;-) I wanted to give you something that would remind you of me. Meet Page Jr. and Noah Jr. the geckos. They like snacks and silence. They wouldn't thrive very well in my house, so I thought they would be better off with you.

Page Boone

Your fairy godmother. (Yes, Hagen called me this morning.)

P.S. The real reason I can't keep them at my house is I always forget to feed things.

With a chuckle, I folded the note and set it next to my laptop. It would be one to save.

"Well, Kent, it looks like I'm the proud owner of two geckos named Page Jr. and Noah Jr."

"Thank goodness they don't eat as much as a goat and aren't as messy as a chicken."

"About time we had something lower maintenance, I agree."

"So, what's your deal with her?" He asked as he leaned forward to study the green geckos.

"I like her. I plan on asking her out soon. If I could just get her to stop sending me things that are alive. But I think the geckos are her parting shot. I spoke with her the last night when I was at her house."

Kent straightened quickly, startling the geckos who scurried to hide behind a faux rock in their home. "You were at her house? You just met her."

"She was babysitting her little brother."

"Oh great, you already met the family. You're too far gone now! Just when I thought I'd found my wingman."

"I've never been your wingman. Besides, I'd rather find one girl worth spending the rest of my life with."

"You always take everything so seriously. It makes me sound so shallow."

"That's because you are Kent." Leaning down, I studied the geckos. The brighter colored gecko would be Page Jr. The paler one would be Noah Jr.

"No need to soften the blow, I guess. That's what friends are for. Well, with friends like these," he gestured to the geckos, "you don't exactly need any enemies. Page is like a wrecking ball around this course."

"She's lively."

"She's something all right. I take back every nice thing I said about her the first day I met her. I should have known she was mayhem waiting to happen when she sent those notes to the kitchen staff."

"She's still their favorite after helping the other day."

Kent nodded glumly. "A shame, really."

I glared at him. "I know she's not your favorite person, but at least pretend to be civil when you're around her."

He stood and rapped his knuckles on my desk. "I'll be civil if she stays away and keeps those animals to herself."

"What exactly made you so upset about her?"

I knew what made him so upset. I also figured it was worth pestering him about since he'd asked her out and been turned down—after I'd made it clear that I was interested in her.

He walked to the window and looked outside. "She's so unprofessional. Sending all of those animals?"

"Huh. What's really bothering you?"

He glanced over his shoulder at me. "She's been the talk of the course. Some of the caddies were placing bets on which of them will take her out on a date first."

I wasn't surprised. She was beautiful, she had a quick sense of humor, and she didn't put up with any crap. "Tell them she's unavailable—because she will be dating their boss."

Kent continued grumbling under his breath as he turned and left the room.

I pulled out my phone and snapped a picture of the geckos on my desk and texted it to Page.

Noah: They're happy to be home.

I tried to get to work approving a few more member applications, but I kept hearing a phantom chime on my phone.

Finally, after I'd had to retype three emails due to my distracted state, I heard my phone chime. It was a full thirty minutes before she texted me back. I'd grown a few gray hairs in that time.

· · ·

Page: They can keep you company when I'm not there.

Noah: I thought you'd died when you didn't text back.

Page: Nope. Just working. Are you glued to your phone? Now I'm wondering if you're capable of not answering your phone immediately.

Noah: I don't have to answer my phone right away.

Page: Coffee or tea?

I tapped my phone against the desk as I tried my hardest not to unlock the screen and answer her question. Sweat started to bead on my forehead due to the effort.

Finally, I unlocked it and texted back.

Noah: Tea. What does that have to do with anything?

Page: Congratulations. You made it a full three minutes before texting back. Addict.

Noah: Know of a cure?

Page: *GIF of a shattered phone*

Noah: The only thing I believe in quitting cold turkey is smoking.

Page: Good to know. Now, how am I going to make you like coffee more?

Noah: Why do I have to like coffee?

Page: Because I work in a coffee shop.

Sign me up. I was going to like coffee if it killed me.

· · ·

Noah: Are you there now?

Page: I work tomorrow morning. I'll make you a coffee believer if you let me.

Noah: I'll think about it.

She texted me the address of the coffee shop, along with the hours she was working. I barely refrained from texting her back. I didn't want to come across as too desperate—especially since I was bordering on stalker mode now. I'd shown up at the art gallery and her house. Granted, she kept showing up here—with animals—but I wanted her to look forward to seeing me, not feel pressured to be around me.

Now I knew what I would be doing the next morning, and it wasn't emailing suppliers.

Chapter Eleven

PAGE

My hands worked on autopilot as I made mochas and cappuccinos. I seamlessly flirted with the regulars; until finally, my favorite person to serve stepped up to the counter.

"Cletus, I thought you were banned from this place."

"Nah," he leaned his cane against the counter. "They don't mind taking my money."

Raising my eyebrows at him, I frothed the milk for his coffee. "You must know the owner very well. Why don't you tell me about him?"

"Nicest guy you'll ever meet."

"Oh, I doubt that."

"Can you think of someone nicer?" Cletus scowled me, and I bit my lip to keep from laughing.

"My dad's pretty nice."

"He must be a saint to put up with you," Cletus observed.

"He's better than my cranky old boss."

"Have you been fired lately?"

I shook my head as I handed him his regular drink.

"Well, you're fired."

Cletus owned the coffee shop.

He reminded me of an ankle-high dog that yips furiously at anything and anyone—all bark, no bite. He fired me at least three times a week. It was very therapeutic for him. I kept showing up, and he kept paying me. He usually tipped on the days he fired me.

Splitting my time working at the coffee shop and the art shop meant I could work a lot of hours. The coffee shop was definitely my favorite. Anytime I could get tips, I was happy to take it. I knew it was past time to get serious about finding a career that I could make a living from and help me afford to travel. With lots of time off. Maybe I should start looking into turning into becoming a gold-digger. It had potential.

Anything that would get me out of my parents' backyard. I loved my little cottage and being close to my family, but their lives were consumed with the twins. Cameron and I stuck together. Maybe I'd take him with me on my next weekend trip. I really needed to take some extended time off so I could take a trip longer than three days.

"I'm going in the back to make a couple of phone calls if you need me."

"Okay." I drew the word out. Cletus never told me what he was doing. He was a terrible communicator, so I felt like he had an ulterior motive for telling me this, but I didn't know why.

He stomped past me and headed to the office in the back.

The next half hour I spent mixing drinks and taking money. When the rush slowed, I mentally added up my tip money to my bank account, wondering if I had enough to make it to Belize.

"Excuse me."

I stopped absentmindedly designing a cruise ship with coffee beans and looked up at the customer.

"I'm here to meet someone by the name of Cletus. Do you know if anyone by that name is here yet?"

The woman standing on the other side of the counter wore a pale blue off-the-shoulder dress with a cream-colored handbag over her shoulder. I'm sure it was expensive. I didn't recognize designer clothes or bags, but I could smell out money. She had a friendly smile. But those weren't the things tripping me up. It was the fact that she was asking for Cletus.

"Ma'am? You want to see Cletus?"

Her smile fell. "Oh, well, I thought he'd asked me to meet him here, but if he's not here—"

I bit the side of my cheek accidentally. "Are you here for something business-related?"

"Not exactly." She shifted her bag to her other shoulder and raised her brown, shaped eyebrows at me.

"You're on a date with him?" I stopped tapping my pen against the counter.

She nodded, and I laughed—loudly. Her cheeks turned red, and I realized that I was embarrassing her by drawing attention to us from the other customers. "I'm sorry," I gasped. "It's just, you're so pretty and polite, and Cletus is —well, Cletus is my favorite grump."

She smiled a little at that. "He can be brusque at first."

"That's a nice way of putting it, that's for sure. Can I make you a cup of something? He's in the back office. He'll probably be out at any moment."

"Something strong and caffeinated sounds wonderful."

"I can take care of that. You'll need it for him."

She smiled and tried passing me a card. I waved her off, then began grinding the coffee beans for her espresso.

"Have you worked here long?" She asked as I stirred in the foamed milk.

"For a couple of years now."

"So, you know Cletus well?"

I nodded while I swirled the caramel around the edge of the porcelain mug.

"Are you a student in town?"

"No, I'm just a wandering soul that can't afford to wander."

She gave me a sympathetic look. "Many of us have been in the same situation, sweetie. You'll figure it out."

"And if you're wondering about my opinion of Cletus, he's a cantankerous, grumpy, overbearing sweetheart that I love. But don't you dare tell him I said that. He'll make my life miserable."

Her smile grew. "That makes me feel better. I have to tell you this is the first time I've gone on a date in years. I'm glad he asked me for coffee. Something casual."

I handed her the cup of coffee. "I hope you enjoy your time here. If it doesn't work out between you and Cletus, at least you got a date and a coffee out of the deal. Which reminds me, I'll have to tell him to buy your coffee from now on."

"Buy who's coffee?" Cletus barked from behind me.

I turned around and reprimanded him. "You kept the pretty lady waiting."

His cheeks flushed, and he ducked his head. He mumbled, "I'm so sorry, Caroline. Business got carried away."

He kept muttering apologies while he slipped around the end of the counter. It was cute to see him so embarrassed. I didn't think Cletus could exhibit any other emotion other than testiness.

They walked to the back corner of the shop, sitting

down on an empty leather couch together, stealing embarrassed looks at each other.

It was so strange to see people their age dating, to see the push and pull of trying to get to know each other, wanting to impress their date, and always conscious of their actions.

The next hour, I spent serving coffee and watching Cletus and Caroline. I even had enough time to stencil their initials on a paper napkin. I'd save it for them and gift it to them on their wedding day…

Caroline told me goodbye before she left, and Cletus grumped at me for a few minutes after he escorted her out the door. Overall, I think he liked her a lot. I'd have to find out how he met her later because a line had formed, and I found myself swamped for the next fifteen minutes. Working quickly, I spun back and forth filling cups, grinding the coffee, steaming milk. Tanya, my annoying and useless coworker, managed to get in the way more than help. In spite of that, each cup was delivered quickly and with a smile for the tippers. By the time I had helped almost all of them, my head was spinning from turning around so much.

"Karen!" I called as I set a nonfat, dairy-free, sugar-free, decaf, and happiness-free caramel mocha on the counter.

Karen took her drink and went to sit down with her friend. I turned around to help the next customer and wheezed. It was Noah.

"What—" I cleared my throat. "Can I get for you?"

"What's wrong with your voice?"

So much for acting unsurprised. "It's the opera lessons."

He looked confused for a minute, and it was adorable. I had to keep myself busy, or I was going to ask him out right then. I emptied the punch card stand and pretended to be straightening it.

"Do you know what you want to drink?"

"How about peppermint tea?"

I glanced around to double-check that I was still in the coffee shop. I was. "You realize this is a coffee shop, right?"

He shoved his hands in his pockets. "Most coffee shops serve tea, too."

I scowled at him. "There's something wrong about going to a coffee shop and ordering tea."

His form-fitting jacket stretched across his chest when he shrugged. "I'm not a huge fan of coffee."

Interesting. Well, I liked to think of myself as a missionary with one goal in mind. Convert the coffee-free people to the delights and wonders of caffeine addiction. And trust me, I take that mission seriously. Just call me Mother Teresa.

"Give me a minute, and I'll make you one."

"But-"

"Trust me; you'll love it." I didn't smile because I only smiled at customers who tipped. The more they paid, the more I smiled. It was my version of fair-trade coffee.

"I'm sorry."

"It's okay; not everyone is born loving coffee. Some people have to grow in their love for it."

I heard a short chuckle, but I forced myself to pay attention to what I was doing. I added white chocolate and raspberry next.

"That's not what I meant. I meant, I'm sorry you had to part with Page Jr. and Noah Jr. But I need you to promise me something."

"Promise what?" I took longer than necessary to snap the lid onto the cardboard cup. "Here you go."

He reached out to take the cup from me, but he

wrapped his hand around mine so that we were holding the cup together. "I need you to promise never to send me a singing telegram again. Kent almost died from embarrassment."

I grinned but said nothing. I needed him to reposition his hand so I could let go of the cup. If I tried to pull away, we'd drop the coffee.

He looked so patient leaning against the counter with his hand wrapped around mine. "I'm waiting."

I narrowed my eyes at him. "I'm not sure it's a promise I can keep. How are Noah and Page?"

"Probably my favorite present ever." He smiled and moved his hand down to the bottom of the cup so I could let go. Not that I wanted to. I wanted nothing more than to hold his hand.

"I'll have to come by and visit them so they don't forget about me," I told him.

"Yes, you will. If you let me have your picture, I could show it to them every day so they'll remember you. How long did you have them?"

I picked up a rag and scrubbed at an imaginary streak on the black counter. "About two hours."

Noah chuckled, and it was as though I could feel it all the way to my toes.

"Hey, I grew very attached in those two hours. It was hard to send them to you."

"Well you could help me take care of them."

"I've never co-parented geckos before."

"I'm sure you and I can figure something out. We'd better grab dinner sometime while we figure out the particulars."

I stopped scrubbing the counter. "Is this a business dinner? Should I bring my lawyer? If I could actually afford one, that is."

Noah rested a hand flat on the countertop in front of me, his face serious. His voice was low when he answered, "No, this wouldn't be related to business. It's purely for pleasure. I would even call it a date."

He reached out and grabbed the rag from my hands, where I'd been twisting it tight enough to rip. He set his coffee cup down on the counter and carefully folded the cloth into a neat square without taking his eyes from mine. "What do you say?"

"Yes. Yup. One hundred percent."

He smiled, and I was pretty sure I was levitating over the coffee bean littered floor.

"You like me," I said to reassure myself that I'd heard him correctly. He wanted to go on a date with me. Me. He'd even seen most of my crazy, and still asked me out.

"Yeah, I like you. Now, you let me know when works for you. I know where I want to take you, if you trust me to plan the date."

Unable to come up with a coherent answer, I simply nodded and smiled.

He tipped his coffee cup towards me and winked.

"I've got to go feed Page Jr. and Noah Jr. Have a great day."

"I will now."

Chapter Twelve

NOAH

Three days after I'd asked Page out on a date, we were finally going out. It might as well have been three months. I planned on taking her to dinner on Magazine Street, then over to the Palace Market Frenchman. I'd have the bonus of an hour-long car ride with her each way.

Walking up to the same house address where I'd ate popcorn and watched movies with Page and Cameron, I knocked on the blue door.

The door opened and Cameron stood there. His face lit up with a smile when he saw me. "Hi, Noah!"

"Hey Cameron, how are you?"

"Good! What are you doing holding flowers?"

"Flowers?" someone called over his shoulder.

Two identical faces peered over his shoulder at me. The girls looked like they were somewhere in the high school age range: the twins I'd heard so much about.

"Who are you?" One of them asked.

"I'm Noah. I'm here to pick up Page for our date. Is she home?"

"Yeah, she's home——"

Another voice calling interrupted us. "Who's at the door?"

A man in his early fifties appeared behind the trio. "Dad, this is Noah," Cameron explained.

The man nodded as if that explained everything. "I'm Andrew."

I leaned past Cameron and the girls to shake Andrew's hand. "Noah. Nice to meet you."

It didn't make sense that I was nervous about meeting him. I was far past being a nervous young boy meeting his girlfriend's dad. Yet I still felt a little nauseous...

"Page is out back." He gestured over his shoulder, then walked away.

And I guess that was the end of introductions. "Out back?"

"Come on; I'll show you." Cameron shoved past his sisters, grabbed my arm, and dragged me around the side of the house. It must be a family trait to grab people and drag them off.

I followed him around the side yard and across a brick walkway that led to a small cottage in the back of the yard. "Page lives here. Mom and Dad wanted her out of the house, so they made a deal with her to live here instead of the main house."

It was such a loaded statement I wasn't sure how to respond. I'd have to ask Page about it. "Thanks for showing me."

"Are you coming back for movie night this week?"

I smiled at the eagerness in his tone. "If it's all right with Page, I'll be there."

"Great!" He gave a quick wave then walked back to the main house. I switched the roses to my left hand so I could knock on the pale pink door.

The small, white cottage had a porch with a table and chair on it. The railing went around the little deck, and there were only two steps up. It felt like I was stepping into a dollhouse.

"Be right there!"

I heard a few thumps and crashes before the door swung open to reveal Page wearing an off the shoulder black lace dress. She had on a pair of high heels that brought her closer to my height. I wouldn't have to bend as far down to kiss her.

"You look beautiful."

She smiled. "You do too. Handsome, I mean. You look handsome."

I held the roses out to her.

"Thank you. Come in while I find something to put these in." She took the roses from me and headed towards the back of the cottage.

Stepping inside, I realized it was only one room. A queen-size bed pushed up against the wall on one side. Easels and a large desk sat on the other side. Paint tubes covered the desk. Clothes piled high on a soft chair.

There was a small bathroom in the back-left corner and a wall of cabinets.

Page rummaged around in the cupboards and finally pulled out a tall vase to put the roses in. She disappeared into the bathroom, and I could hear the water running while she filled the vase. There was a small mini-fridge and a microwave but no other appliances in sight.

I looked at some of her artwork. Unfortunately, I discovered the imitation Picasso's immediately. They were something. I'd never seen anything like them. And I hoped I would never see anything like them again.

I glanced at the sketches propped up on the desk. They were sketches of me. She was good. She made me look attractive—strong, unbendable. She made me look way better than

"You're not wearing a suit! I almost didn't recognize you." She told me as she walked back out and set the flowers in the center of a small round table.

"I hope you don't mind." I gestured to my casual wear.

She walked up to me a ran a hand over the front of my sweater. "No, I don't mind. I think I like casual Noah."

She ironed out a few more imaginary wrinkles while I did my best to keep breathing.

"These must be the Picassos." I jerked my chin in the direction of the paintings.

"Do you like them?"

My throat dried up when I tried to answer. "I've never seen anything like them."

"I have to admit that I struggled with *Guernica*. But I think my best imitation was the *Old Man with a Guitar*." She pointed to one an easel in the kitchen. I had thought it was a woman holding a spoon. Apparently, I was wrong.

She looked at the desk and leaped forward to turn the two sketches of me facedown. "Pretend like you didn't see those." She looped her arm through mine.

"See what?" I winked at her, and she smiled back. "You really enjoy painting, don't you?"

"Painting, sketching. Anything. One of these days, I'm going to pack my art bag and spend a few months touring Europe and adding some culture into my life."

The fact that she wanted to travel wasn't a surprise. "Page, I think you would add culture to European life."

She looked up at me and smiled. "You're probably right."

"You can tell me all about your traveling plans on our date tonight, come on." I unhooked her arm from mine and instead entwined my fingers through hers.

"We have reservations."

"Where?"

"Do you like surprises?"

"Love them."

"Then come on."

During dinner, Page pulled an old receipt and pencil from her purse, then sketched my picture while we chatted and waited for our food. It was incredible. I'd never seen anyone sketch so fast. Her Picasso's might be horrible—heck, I didn't particularly care for the original Picasso's—but her sketches were incredibly detailed. I leaned toward her to get a better look at the picture.

"Hey, why are there little lines by my eyes?"

"Some people call those wrinkles." She smirked while she tapped the pencil against her water glass.

"I don't have wrinkles."

"Fine, they're tiny crinkles."

I tried my best to give her a stern look. "I'm not old enough to be wrinkly."

"How old are you?"

"Thirty-two."

She nodded. "That's the age when the wrinkles come out to play. There's no hiding now."

I leaned close and studied her face. Smooth skin, not a wrinkle or crinkle in sight. "Your turn."

"Hmm?" She began rearranging her silverware.

I reached across the table and pulled the silverware out of her reach. "How old are you?"

"Ages younger. Twenty-six." She winked.

I slipped the receipt out from under her fingertips and studied the picture.

"This is amazing."

"You think so?" She asked softly. I didn't know she was capable of speaking in a soft voice.

"I think so. You are an incredible sketch artist."

I could barely sign my name on a bank slip, much less draw someone's face on a wrinkled receipt.

The waiter served our dinner, and I carefully folded the picture and tucked it in my wallet.

It was the first time I'd gone to Lilette, and it did not disappoint. After dinner, we made our way to the Palace Market and wandered around the booths.

Page reached out and slipped her hand into mine as we perused the art. We talked about anything and everything. Feeling her hand in mine as we walked was about the best thing I could ask for.

Our conversation inevitably drifted toward work.

"So, your grandpa gave you a golf course. Is this something you've thought about since you were young?"

I chuckled. "No, I never thought I'd own a golf course. It was more like it was handed to me."

"You must have large hands," she teased. "But I get the feeling you're not happy about it."

Talking about my grandfather was probably one of my least favorite topics. I didn't want to bring in the family drama on our first date. If I wanted to keep dating her, it would probably be wise to refrain from ever mentioning my grandfather.

"Eh, I'll figure it out."

She nudged my arm with her elbow. "Why don't you do something else if you don't like it?"

"I think it comes down to the fact that I want to prove to myself that I can turn it around. I love making something succeed."

"Aha, so you like a challenge." She let go of my hand and linked her arm through mine. "What other things have you done?"

"I created a chain of cross-fit gyms. Started a few coffee shops"

Her hand squeezed my bicep as she said, "I can tell."

"In college, I created a bike delivery service. I paid my entire tuition with that business."

She leaned back and looked at me. "So—you're actually good at making money with your businesses?"

I nodded. "They usually do well. I still own those businesses and make a nice little income from them. Nothing flashy."

She laughed, "I have a feeling you're being modest. Why is The Garden struggling then?"

"Let's just say there's a reason my grandfather got out of the business when he did."

"Did he retire or something?"

"Something like that," I muttered under my breath, but Page heard me and laughed.

"Come on, tell me about it. I'll tell you mine if you tell me yours." She winked.

Shaking my head, I decided it'd be better to answer her. "My grandfather and grandmother are divorced now. He left her to marry another woman, but he still lives and breathes to cause her grief. He's always trying to make her jealous by showing off his latest girlfriend or wife. None of his relationships last long. He's a terrible businessman who wasted away his money, my grandma's money, and anyone's money who was stupid enough to invest with him."

"He's a bitter old man who's bad at money—I still don't get why you own the golf course."

"I'm getting to that. Be patient."

She gave me a sheepish grin.

"The Garden was one of his 'great investment opportunities' that started going under fast. To keep in good standing with some of his business contacts, he claimed he needed to retire because of his age and health problems. He passed it on to yours truly as part of my "inheritance." He'll get to blame its failure and bankruptcy on me, all the while appearing like a benevolent man who only wanted to give his grandson a leg up in the world."

"Why didn't you say no?"

I shrugged, "I have this terrible urge to succeed when others want me to fail. He expects me to fail, so I guess I'm stuck with the golf course until it's thriving."

I stopped walking and looked into her eyes. She had a mischievous look in her eye. "So, how are we going to stick it to him?"

"We?" I liked the sound of that.

"Yes, we. We, Page and Noah the humans, and also Page and Noah the geckos."

"I think we should leave Page Jr. and Noah Jr. out of the whole thing. They're too young to understand."

She smiled and squeezed my hand. "So, why did your grandfather pick on you? Why didn't he leave the golf course to someone else in the family? Any siblings or parents?"

"My sister has four kids and is a pediatrician. My

mother quit her job as a district attorney and started working at her local library. She loves it and says she never wants to quit. She has time to spend with the grandkids now."

Page bit her lip, and I braced myself for the question I knew was coming next. "What about your father?"

I swallowed and answered—it was the question I dreaded most. "My father passed away when I was eighteen."

She gasped. I prepared myself for the usual pitying look and change of subject that people did. Instead, she released my hand and slipped her arms around my middle and hugged me. She squeezed tight—as if she could fix the gaping hole in my life. Oddly enough, it felt nice—even as I remembered my father. Fourteen years and there was still an ache. Feeling her warmth wrapped around me made that ache in my heart ease. I missed my dad, and I always would, but I couldn't argue that it felt nice to have Page hugging me.

I wrapped my arms around her and held her as curious looks from passersby bored into us. It felt like we were the center of a flash mob, but I didn't want to move anytime soon.

After a few moments, I said, "You know, you're the best hugger I've ever met."

"Of course, I am. I like hugging people," she said as she pulled back. "I seriously looked into becoming a professional cuddler, but Kylie talked me out of it."

I wasn't sure I liked the thought of her hugging a bunch of other people. "I don't know Kylie, but I like her already."

She squeezed my arm as she continued. "A hug might not fix anything, but it makes things more tolerable."

"I disagree."

She leaned farther back and raised her eyebrows, "You don't?"

"No, I don't." I brushed the back of my fingers against her slender neck. "I think your hugs could fix just about anything."

I pressed a kiss against her forehead then turned us to walk through the displays again. I kept her tucked close to my side—a small smile stayed on her face.

A few minutes later, she spoke up. "I have an idea for the golf course."

"Oh, really." I tried to sound excited.

"Do you want me to tell you about it?"

"If it involves single women or farm animals, then no," I stated firmly.

She bit her lip and pretended to think about it. "Single men, then."

I glared at her, and she laughed. "Actually, I was thinking about you doing an art, wine, and golf night. It would broaden your demographic."

She spent the next thirty minutes excitedly telling me about her plans for an art night that I could host at The Garden. She pointed out several local artists she knew and told me that she could arrange for all the artists to be there. She told me about her cousin who was a marketer—the same cousin marrying Hagen Raglund.

"Well, what do you think?"

"I think it's a great idea."

Her eyes shone as she looked up at me. "You think so?"

"Yes, I do. Do you know someone who's organized something like this before?"

"How hard could it be? I'll do it for free, and you won't have to worry about hiring anyone."

Of course, she would offer to do it for free. She was like the superhero of golf courses. A little rough around the edges, but well-intentioned. Her idea wasn't half bad. It would open it up to a broader clientele.

As we left the gallery, she continued listing her ideas. I don't think she even noticed that we were walking down the street, or that the sun had set long ago.

The streetlamps added golden highlights to her glossy brown hair. Her heart shaped lips moved rapidly as she explained how she would decorate for an art and wine night at The Garden. Her face glowed with excitement as she went into detail about why forest green would be perfect.

I couldn't care less whether it was forest green or regular green. Watching her excitement over the event was enough for me to let her do anything she wanted.

Her right hand waved through the air as she spoke. Her animated gestures made me unnaturally excited about the art and wine night.

I tugged her hand when we reached my car, pulling her to a stop.

"So, what do you think?" she asked eagerly.

"All right. I'm game."

"Really?"

I smiled. "Yes, really. I think an art night would be perfect to showcase the restaurant now that I have a decent chef. Hopefully, we'll have the new menu finalized by then. I like your ideas."

She beamed up at me. "You like my ideas. I'll get started planning everything right away. Oh, look! We're already at the car."

We'd been standing next to the car for five minutes. She wouldn't win any points for being observant.

I reached past her to open the door for her, accidentally bumping into her and knocking her off balance. Wrapping an arm around her waist, I pulled her close to me. "Sorry about that," I apologized hoarsely as I looked down into her big brown eyes.

She tilted her head toward mine, and I lowered my forehead to hers.

"I'd like to kiss you," I whispered. We were standing on the sidewalk on the outskirts of the French Quarter. But Page made me feel like we were the only two people in the universe.

She didn't answer me. Instead, she leaned forward and pressed her soft lips against mine. Her slender, strong hands steadied herself on my shoulders.

A tingle ran up my spine as she laced her hands behind my neck. Parting my lips, inviting her in, I threaded my fingers through her silky hair.

She kissed the same way she did everything else in life —with fervency and charm.

It was as though she infused life into my soul. All the business opportunities in the world couldn't compare to this feeling. The thrill of success had nothing on Page Boone's kisses.

Chapter Thirteen

PAGE

"Good morning, Caroline. Here's your coffee. I added an extra shot this morning since Cletus seems especially grumpy today."

Her eyes sparkled as I handed her an espresso in a green mug. Cletus and Caroline regularly met at the coffee shop and sat in the back corner either on the couch or at the small table beneath the window.

I was pro-Caroline. As I'd quickly discovered in the last week, she was one of those people that was sweet to everyone. When she called me 'sweetie' it was a term of endearment—unlike my grandmother, Mimi, who would only call you 'sweetie' if she was ready to kill you.

"Thank you, darling."

She winked and headed to the table where Cletus had his wrinkled hands wrapped around a mocha. I'd made him a decaf today. He didn't need any more pep. I watched as Cletus' face broke into a wrinkled grin as Caroline sat down across from him. His face looked so different. So... happy.

I didn't know anything about Cletus' past—he'd never

mentioned it. But grief is a cloud that's entirely recogniz-able in people who have experienced it. Some people hide that cloud with other emotions. Some try to pretend like that cloud is never there. Others, like Cletus, carry the cloud in their arms—afraid to let it go.

I swiped at the mist in the corner of my eyes. It must be getting close to my time of the month—that must be why I was getting so emotional at seeing Cletus happy on his little date.

I focused on cleaning the pastry display case until the bell above the door sounded.

The next customer was strong, handsome, and hope-fully, mine.

"Good morning," Noah smiled as he stepped in front of the counter. "I enjoyed last night."

I could have sworn I was blushing. My cheeks felt warm, and I had an overwhelming urge to bury my face behind the scone display.

"I enjoyed last night, too," I answered. His smile grew even more at that. "What are you doing here this morning?"

"I know this great barista who can make anyone like coffee. I thought I might give her another chance to convert me. What do you think?"

I grabbed a mug off the shelf. "I think I could do that."

He stepped over to the side counter and watched me as I worked. "What are the chances this barista might go on another date with me?"

"I'd say pretty good. Only because you're a good kiss-er." I winked and waggled my eyebrows at him.

It was his turn to blush as he glanced around.

"Are you free tonight?"

"I thought you had to do some work at the golf course tonight."

"I thought we might grab dinner together again. I can do work like that at home, anyway."

"I would love to go on a date with you again."

He cleared his throat. "I actually was hoping I could convince you to come with me to eat dinner at the golf course in a couple of weeks. The new chef is working on the menu right now. He's still settling on a few things, but we plan on doing a trial run of the menu in two weeks. Which means there's lots of taste-testing that needs to happen. I need a second opinion. What do you say?"

I'd never been asked to be a taste tester before, but that was a job I wouldn't mind. "Yes. Good food and good company? Count me in."

He grinned as I handed him his mug full of coffee—not tea. He turned to glance around the coffee shop. I took off my apron and hat, reminded Tanya—the girl sitting on the stool in the corner—to get off of the phone and take a turn at the counter. I grabbed my iced coffee from the fridge and walked around the counter to stand next to Noah. He was staring at Cletus, who sat in the corner with his girlfriend, her back to us.

"Who's that in the corner?"

"That's my cranky boss."

"Who's that with him?"

I shrugged and took a sip of my coffee. "Believe it or not, Cletus has a girlfriend. She's nice. I'm not sure how he landed her."

"I think I do." Noah's smile reminded me of Cameron whenever he beat me at Monopoly.

He made his way towards Cletus and Caroline's table, and I followed behind, curious what he was up to.

"Grandma, imagine finding you here." Noah rested a hand on the back of Caroline's chair. Caroline turned to face us, flashed a guilty look at Noah, then recovered with a big smile as she stood up and hugged him.

I couldn't stop staring. I'd been chatting it up with Noah's grandma. I'd been making her four-shot coffees— he was probably going to kill me.

"How are you dear?" She pulled his head down and kissed him on the cheek. "I didn't know you came to this coffee shop."

"Are you going to introduce me to your friend?"

Caroline blushed and rested her hand on Cletus' shoulder. "Noah, I'd like you to meet Cletus. My boyfriend."

Cletus choked on a sip of coffee, Noah was trying hard not to laugh, and I was grinning. It was nice to see Cletus so discomfited. If he didn't know he was dating Caroline, he did now.

Noah held out his hand to Cletus, who hesitantly shook it.

"I hadn't realized you knew my grandson," Caroline said to me.

"I hadn't realized you were his grandma," I answered.

"Grandma, Page and I are dating."

"Oh, how wonderful!" Caroline patted my arm as she sat down again. "We'll have to go on a double date sometime."

Cletus choked on some more coffee. There must have been something stuck in his throat. I really should remind him to go see his doctor more regularly.

"It was good to see you grandma—and to meet your new boyfriend."

Cletus looked green, while Noah's eyes had the twinkle I loved so much.

I slipped my hand into the crook of Noah's elbow, and we walked back to the front of the shop. "You have a grandma!"

"Of course, I have a grandma. I've mentioned her before."

"Wait—oh! She was the grandma who was married to—"

"Yes. She was married to Alec, who left me the golf course."

Racking my brain, I tried to remember the details of everything he'd told me about his grandma over the course of our date. "But he left her for someone else."

"Right."

"But now he's mad that she's seeing someone."

"Yup."

"And that someone is Cletus?"

"Probably."

I sighed. "You're full of conversation today, aren't you?"

He grinned. "Sorry, it surprised me to see them here. We've heard about this mystery-man, but grandma didn't want any of us to scare him away, so she hasn't introduced us yet."

"You? Scare someone away? That's hilarious. You tried that with me, look where that got you."

He studied me as he took a sip of his coffee. He was quick to school his grimace. "You're right. It got me a gorgeous girlfriend who's fun to be around."

I bit the corner of my lip and raised my eyebrows. "Oh, so I'm your girlfriend now?"

"We've been on a date. We've watched Indiana Jones together." He lowered his voice. "I've kissed you. It's definitely official."

"You know, I think you and I remember our little movie night differently. I remember you coming over, specifically to get mad about the goat."

"No, not the goat. All the single ladies. I didn't need

help to find a single lady. I'd already found mine." He drained the last of his cup then set it in the bin on the side counter. "I've got to get to work, but I'll see you later, okay? I'll pick you up at your house again."

"That sounds great." I leaned closer to him and kissed him on the cheek. He smiled and blushed as he headed out the door.

It was going to be a good day.

For the next couple of weeks, I felt like I could walk on water. I spent every spare moment with Noah. He was working long hours at The Garden, but we managed to fit in dates on lunch breaks or Sundays. If we weren't together, then we were texting. I learned he really *was* the fastest texter on earth. Or maybe he dictated them while he worked; I'd have to ask him.

I'd been looking forward to the taste testing night ever since he first mentioned it. Noah and I were the only ones sitting in The Garden's restaurant. We'd just finished sampling everything that the new chef had made. Noah's new chef, Mason Walsh, was amazing. It was the first time I'd eaten at the golf course since the day I killed the snake. The old menu wasn't even comparable to the new one.

Mason had made us sample dishes of all types. Salads, appetizers, soups, steak, and, of course, dessert. I was too full to ever walk again. Mason was a dreamboat with those skills. Noah explained that his friend Xavier had helped him find Mason.

If I had the money, I would have tried to hire him out from under Noah to be my personal chef.

"Do you think he'd be willing to cook for me if I offered him room and board?" I asked Noah as I licked the caramel glaze off of my fork.

Noah chuckled as he glanced at the kitchen door then back to me. "No. Besides, I'm not sure how I'd feel about you sharing your small space with him."

I scooted forward in my seat. "Would it bother you? If I had a guy for a roommate?"

"Honestly?" He set his napkin down on the table.

"No, be dishonest."

He chuckled and tried to iron the crumpled-up napkin flat on the table. "Honestly, it would bother me."

"Because you don't trust me?" I didn't know why I was spoiling for a fight tonight. Maybe restless energy. I hadn't traveled anywhere

"No, I don't own you. I don't want to make your decisions for you. That's on you. I will not be the boyfriend who micromanages every move you make."

I unfolded my arms and reached across the table to run my fingers over the back of his hand. He caught them and gently massaged my hand in his. "Why would it bother you?"

He glanced up, his piercing blue eyes prying me open with a look. "I'd be jealous. If you had a roommate, they'd get to see you in the mornings before breakfast. They'd get to see you morning and night. They would know if you slept in matching pajamas. They would know how grumpy you are before you get your morning coffee. And I would be jealous of that."

I squeezed his hand. "First off, I don't want a roommate. I just want good food to appear on my little breakfast table miraculously. Secondly, sometimes I wear matching pajamas, sometimes I wear sweats and a t-shirt, and sometimes I wear nothing at all. I'm abominable to be around in the mornings until I have two cups of coffee, so don't expect a good morning greeting if we meet in the early hours."

"Nothing at all, huh?" He grinned, and I lightly smacked the back of his hand, careful not to send any plates or flatware flying into the air. Chuckling, he said, "Well, if I can ever get you to go on a jog with me, I'll bring you two coffees first."

I laughed. Then I laughed some more. "You're the funniest thing. Me—go jogging."

He shook his head at me. "Not much of a jogger?"

"Nope. I like being active. I like going on a hike and seeing new scenery. I even like beating my little sisters at tennis. But if you ever see me jogging down the road, please pull over and help me, because there's something chasing me."

Noah threw his head back and laughed. "I don't know if anything would dare chase you, Page. You'd probably give it the scare of its life."

I shrugged. "There was that time when I was in New York, and someone tried to rob me."

Noah flinched then slammed his elbows on the table. "What did you say?"

Waving a hand through the air, I took a sip of my wine. "Don't stress out about it. It was nothing. By the time we were through, I'd earned five bucks for my efforts."

Noah shook his head. "Wait. You robbed him?"

"No, of course not. I have scruples. But I pointed out to him that he could have easily traumatized me, and he owed me for putting up with his shenanigans."

Noah rubbed a hand over his face. "Were you alone?"

"Yes, that time Jenny was at the hotel sleeping."

"That time? You mean you've been robbed more than once?"

Maybe it wasn't the best story to be telling Noah. He didn't seem to appreciate the gist of the story. He was too focused on mechanics.

"Where would you travel to if you could go anywhere?" I asked him.

He reached across the table and latched onto my arm. "Were you robbed before?"

His hand squeezed my arm firmly—but not painfully. When I looked him in the eye, he then pulled his hand back across the small table. He folded them together, resting them against his abdomen while he gave me a stern look. He must mean business.

"It's part of traveling and exploring. It's not a big deal. That's why you never carry a bunch of cash on you."

"Can you do something for me?" His eyebrows drew together.

"Sure."

"Can you promise you'll never travel alone?"

I couldn't tell if he was serious or not. I'd just added Nepal to my travel list the night before. No one wanted to go with me. Jenny said she had some stuff going on and wasn't sure which trips she could commit to.

"I appreciate your concern—I really do. I think it's sweet. But I plan on doing a lot of traveling by myself."

"What does that mean?"

"It means that my traveling partner said she's busy. Kylie's getting married. Mack and Jordan don't like to travel. So that leaves me. And I still have a lot of places to see."

"You have to promise me you won't go alone. It's not safe."

"You know, Noah, if I wanted the Dad speech, I'd go home and hang out with my parents."

Shaking his head, he pressed his lips together. "I'm not joking around here, Page. You could have been hurt. This is serious."

I stood up and tossed my napkin onto the table. "Then I guess I'll go home. I don't want to spend my time with someone who doesn't believe I can make good decisions."

Snatching my purse off the back of the chair, I stomped out of the empty restaurant, through the front lobby and out the large doors. It was another muggy night, and the mosquitoes were already humming.

The door slammed open and heavy footsteps sounded on the sidewalk behind me. I continued walking toward the road. I would walk home if he thought he could tell me how I could and couldn't travel.

A car pulled alongside me, and the window rolled down. "Page, get in the car. We need to talk."

"I'm mad," I informed him—just in case my crossed arms and angry steps weren't enough for him to notice.

Noah chuckled and stopped the car, getting out to open the passenger side door for me. He gave me his best puppy dog face.

"Let's talk," he said in a cajoling tone.

I scoffed, "Those are the worst words in the English language. No pleasant conversation comes after those words."

I stepped closer to him and glared. He opened his arms.

The horrible man knew I couldn't resist him.

I stepped into him and wrapped my arms around his waist. I pressed my face into his chest.

"I was mad at the idea of someone trying to hurt you," he mumbled against my hair.

"Well, don't be so controlling!" I ran my hands up and down his back, feeling the corded muscles that stretched up his back and over his shoulders.

"I'm not controlling."

I leaned back and studied his earnest face.

"All right, fine, I am a little controlling." He rubbed small circles on my back.

I pinched his side—no fat to pinch, only skin.

"Ouch! Hey, I'm not that controlling. I'm concerned."

"Well, you don't have to concern yourself with me."

"Too late. I'm already concerned."

I inhaled the scent of him. Cinnamon and a hint of men's shaving lotion. "Why are you so concerned about my traveling? People travel solo all the time." His hands running up and down my back made me forget why I was mad at him. It wasn't fair.

His hoarse voice said, "Because I love you."

The words echoed into the night and I stopped breathing, afraid that if I started again it would erase the spoken words.

I leaned back to look him in the eye.

He visibly swallowed and lowered his forehead to mine. "I love you, Page. I would go crazy if anything happened to you. Don't you know that?"

I locked my hands together behind his waist. "You mean that?"

"I mean that. I wouldn't say it unless I meant it—I know without a doubt that I love you."

Forget fighting about my travel habits. He loved me. He said the L-word. Out loud. To my face. He seemed like the type of guy to wait until at least the six-month mark.

After taking a steadying breath, I said, "I promised myself that I wouldn't fall in love until my thirtieth birthday. There's so much to see and do in life. I didn't want to be tied down."

His brow furrowed. "Love doesn't tie you down. It bonds you with somebody—somebody to be with you anywhere, someone to support you, not hold you back."

Licking my lips, I spoke, "The night you walked into the art gallery, I started to fall. I kept reminding myself that I was too young to fall in love, but that didn't seem to stop it. You're kind, you're funny, you're steady, you're dedicated. You've trusted me to try something new. With that trust you've sparked an idea in my mind, a way to create my place in the world. You're more than I deserve, and I love you too."

He drew in a deep breath. "You mean that?"

I pinched his side again and tried to imitate his low voice. "I wouldn't say it unless I meant it."

He smiled down at me. "I'm sorry I made you mad. I'm sorry I seemed controlling. I want to support you and love you—and keep you safe."

I nodded as I pulled his head down to mine, pressing my lips against his. I'd just have to kiss that fear out of him.

"We would have loved to continue as members at The Garden, but after speaking with Alec, I think it's best we move on to somewhere we're sure will be sustainable," the man on the other end of the phone explained to me.

"Mr. Ross, I appreciate the years you have spent here at the golf course. It's been great to get to know you over the past couple of months, and I respect your decision. But I have to ask, why do you think it won't be a sustainable golf course?" Might as well find out what the rumors were saying, so I'd know what I was dealing with. I had a pretty good guess I knew who to blame; my grandfather.

"You know I hate to talk about money..."

Oliver Ross loved to talk about money.

"...But your grandfather explained to me how you've nearly bankrupted The Garden in the short time you've been running it. I had hoped to be a long-term member there, but I think I'll be moving my business over to Sandy Pines."

I gritted my teeth in frustration. I'd been right.

I told Ross goodbye, then turned back to Alisha and Mandy, who were helping me sort through old and new membership files at the front desk.

"You can archive Oliver Ross' membership file." I slipped my phone into my pocket and turned to go.

"You know he's been here, right?"

Turning around, I found Mandy leaning against the counter, resting her head in her hands.

"Who's been here?" I asked her.

"Alec Dunaway. He was here with a woman."

I groaned. I knew he didn't want me to succeed; but I hadn't expected him to take an active part in making me fail. Thank goodness business was picking up in spite of his efforts.

"Next time he shows up, please call me right away."

She nodded and motioned to Alisha over her shoulder. "We'll make sure everyone knows that."

"Thank you." Walking away, I made a conscious effort not to storm off. Just because my grandfather was causing problems, didn't mean I had to lose my temper.

As I walked past the restaurant, I glanced inside. The brunette from singles-mingle night was there again. She'd been coming regularly for the last month. When her eyes landed on me, she leaped out of her seat, knocking her water glass over.

"Hi Noah!" She waved. "Do you have time for a drink?"

I forced a smile. "Busy right now, but thanks."

I practically ran upstairs to my office and pulled my phone from my pocket. Page had texted while I was talking with Oliver.

Page: Why do some people have to be so lame?

Noah: Bad day at work?

Page: What gave me away?

Noah: Tell me about it. I've had a long day too.

Page: Let's talk it over while we eat popcorn and watch a movie with Cameron tonight.

Noah: It's a deal.

"You came!" Cameron shouted as he opened the front door to his parents' house. Unfortunately, with how much I'd been working, I hadn't been able to make it to a Cameron/Page hang out night since before we started dating.

I passed him the ice cream container but kept the flowers to hand to Page myself.

"I didn't want to miss out on movie night. What are we watching tonight?"

I toed off my dress shoes wishing I had taken the time to go home and change into jeans. But since I was excited to see Page, I didn't want to waste an hour for a pair of jeans.

Page stood at the stovetop, stirring a pot. She turned and smiled. "You brought flowers!"

"And ice cream," Cameron added as he stuck it in the freezer.

Page stepped away from the stove and leaned up on

her tiptoes, giving me a quick kiss. "You're just in time for dinner. I'm making my specialty."

"You can cook? Why didn't I know about this before?"

She nodded and gestured to the pot behind her. "Best box mac and cheese you'll ever eat."

I laughed as I traded her the flowers for the spoon. She found a vase in the lower cabinet while I stirred the noodles. "Is it supposed to be sticking to the bottom?"

Her eyes widened. "Of course, it's called crusty mac and cheese for a reason."

I shook my head and pulled the pot off the burner. I glanced at Cameron. "How do you feel about bowling and pizza?"

"Really?" Cameron asked. He headed straight to the door and slipped on a pair of tennis shoes.

"Oh, come on! My mac and cheese is not that bad!" Page protested. She set the flowers in a vase then jerked the spoon out of my hand. She vigorously scraped the bottom of the pot with the metal spoon.

"You're so right, it isn't that bad," I reassured her as a few black noodles flew out of the pan, sizzling on the stovetop.

"Hush up, you. You've never tried my mac and cheese." She smacked my chest with the spoon as she leaned past me to shut off the stove. "I'll bring you mac and cheese for lunch tomorrow. Then you can eat your heart out, Noah Dunaway."

She slipped her feet out of a pair of fuzzy slippers and into a pair of shoes. She sniffed. "I guess we could handle some pizza right now." She opened the door and slammed it behind herself.

Cameron looked at me and shrugged. "She's a little touchy when it comes to cooking. She really wanted to make you dinner, but she's an awful cook."

"You can say that again."

We went to a bowling alley and ate greasy pizza—the only food that can be disgusting and wonderful at the same time. Page decided she wasn't too mad at me since the macaroni really had turned black. I suspected she liked the idea of me making a fool of myself at a bowling alley—especially since she'd been teasing me about wearing bowling shoes with a suit.

We sat at a small table—that I didn't dare look at closely—while we watched Cameron perfect his spin-and-throw technique with a bright-pink bowling ball.

"He's a fun kid."

Page nodded as she took a big bite of pepperoni pizza. "He'll do."

I smiled at that, knowing she adored him from the short time we'd been dating. "Obviously, that's why you live in the tiny house. You can't stand your brother."

One of her eyebrows twitched. "You're right, of course. I wanted to get as far from him as possible. That's why I live in the backyard."

"Why do you live in the backyard? I know you love to travel. I guess I'm surprised that you're not living in a flat in the middle of Paris." I took a bite of my pizza, the cheese stretching away from the slice.

Page rested her chin in her hand as she watched Cameron attempt to throw the bowling ball backward. "I enjoy hanging out with him. Besides, Mom and Dad are busy with the twins."

"Wait—aren't they in high school?"

Page nodded as she picked off another piece of pepperoni and ate it. "They have lots of activities they're involved in. Mom and Dad are always helping them with different things. They don't have a lot of time left for Cameron. That's why I pick him up from school."

There was something messed up with that. "That isn't right."

"What?" she asked as she took a drink of her coke.

"That's not your job."

"I know." She groaned. Then she lowered her voice, "I know—but it's my parents, and I love them. I love Cameron too."

I couldn't imagine my mother taking advantage of me the way Page's parents were. They needed to raise their own kids—all of them. "I don't see what's tying you down here. I think a lot of this pressure you put on yourself. If you talked with your parents, it might surprise you to find that they would support you."

She looked down at the pizza and focused on stacking olive slices on top of each other. "Yeah. But if I talk to them, then I won't have any excuses."

"Excuses?"

She nodded as her olive tower toppled over. "I don't know what to do with my life. If I stay there, I never have to put myself out there and discover what to do. I can be happy hanging out with my brother, taking trips on the weekends, and never worrying about carving out my own place in the world."

It didn't feel like the right time to say anything, so I didn't.

"The truth is, I'm scared. Scared to try. Scared that I won't find something I like. Scared I won't fit in."

"You won't fit in."

She glanced up at me, her mouth parted in surprise.

"Do you want to know why?"

"Maybe not."

I leaned forward and grabbed her hand, hoping to help her see what I saw in her. "I'll tell you anyway. You weren't made to fit in. No matter where you go, you're going to stand out. You're energetic. You're unafraid in the moment. You're kind, thoughtful, and overly generous with live animals."

She laughed at that.

"You don't have to fit in. I don't want you to change. I love every part about you."

"I'm such a loser. I'm twenty-six years old and living in my parents' backyard."

"And look at everything you've done! You've travelled all over the United States, you've taught yourself to sketch." I left out the painting part, hoping she wouldn't notice. "You've invested in a coffee shop—don't look so shocked, Cletus told Grandma, and Grandma told me. No wonder he can't fire you—you own a share of it."

She focused her attention on the olives again. "It seemed like a good use of my money. I feel like I'm ready to find something that I love. It has been so much fun planning this art night for you. It's made me realize it's time to find a job I love like that—even find a place that will be all my own."

"When are you moving out?"

Pressing her might not be the best idea, but she talked about her dreams all the time. She needed to do something about them.

"Hey, now. When you say it like that, it sounds like I live in my childhood bedroom. I have my own house, thank you very much."

"It's microscopic—and I know you don't like it."

"Fine. Since you know me so well, what would I like?" She was getting huffy now, but that was okay. I didn't mind her being mad at me, as long as she finally did something that she wanted to. She was scared, and I wanted to help her. I knew she had big dreams—she just needed someone to support her in them.

"I think you need time to go travel the way you would like to. I think you need someone who will support you in the job that you love. Someone who can encourage you even if it seems scary."

She sniffed. "I don't know if you're making me cry or if it's the pepperoni."

"Definitely the pepperoni."

"Why do you have to be so observant?"

"Because I care about you, and I want you to be happy."

She leaned across the table to wipe a little pizza sauce off my face. "Let's stop talking about my problems. Let's talk about yours—they're much more interesting. How are things at the golf course?"

I cleared my throat then took a sip of my lemonade. "What do you mean how is the course?"

She narrowed her eyes at me. She didn't seem fooled by my innocent voice. "You still need more members, don't you?"

"We're beginning to grow. You don't have to worry about it. No more mascots, right?"

She pressed her lips together and raised her eyebrows at me. "I was sure I'd doomed the golf course that day. That's why I felt so guilty over killing Lucifer."

I laughed. "I still can't believe you sent me a one-legged chicken to make up for it."

She gave me a mischievous grin. "I still can't believe I talked Kylie into hauling a goat in the back of her car."

"You didn't even use your car?"

She winked. "And have the smell of billy-goat stuck in it? No, thank you."

Chuckling, I shook my head. "I hope I get to meet this Kylie someday."

"Oh, you will. It's inevitable if you stick around long enough."

"I plan on sticking around." It was my turn to wink at her.

"And now that you've tried to change the subject let's get back to talking about the golf course. How bad is it?" She reached across the table and squeezed my hand. "It's okay if you don't want to talk about it, but I have the art night all planned for when you're ready for it."

I flipped my hand over to hold hers. "It's okay. I enjoy talking to you. I guess it's a little embarrassing to admit that we haven't been growing as fast as I'd like. I'm trying to pull us out of the hole, but it takes time to gain that traction. We hired on better staff which will help in the long run, but it means our finances took another hit after payday this month."

"So, you're saying if you had some extra money right now, you'd be fine?"

"Maybe. Probably. But it will all work out in the end. Either our renovations and restaurant trials will be worth it, or I'll be forced to try something else."

"You'll fix it. I know you will." She stood up and

leaned over the table to plant a quick kiss on my forehead, then my lips.

"Gross." Cameron plopped onto the seat next to me. "Nobody wants to see old people kiss."

"Old people?" Page asked as she wrapped an arm around his neck. "Are you 'old people' too?"

"Oh, no!" Cameron wailed and laughed at the same time as Page landed a smacking kiss on his cheek. They both dissolved into giggles as they talked about which was more disgusting: kisses or bowling alley floors.

Chapter Fifteen

PAGE

"Here's your coffee." I passed a mug across the counter to Caroline who was there for her morning date with Cletus.

It had been a week since bowling with Noah. I'd officially quit at Carlotta's, which was fine. Lottie didn't seem upset about it and was still happy to help by lending paintings for the art and wine night at The Garden. My tiny house was bursting at the seams with boxes of décor for the night. I wanted it to be perfect.

Noah was happy to leave all of the decorating to me, and he was genuinely excited for the art night. I was still worried about him with how much he was working. But the good news was, he picked an official date for the art night and was already advertising for it.

"Thank you, dear." Caroline dropped some cash in the tip jar, and I smiled at her. She didn't leave. Instead, she rested her large purse on the counter and took a sip of her coffee. "You're dating my grandson."

It wasn't a question.

"Yes."

"That's wonderful. Noah's such a sweetheart, and I've been worried that he hasn't made enough time in life for the important things."

"The important things?"

"Oh, you know, family, friends—girlfriends. I've been worried about him."

I leaned a hip against the counter. "What exactly worried you about him?"

She wrapped her slender, veined hands around the white mug. She glanced behind her as though Noah might be lurking there. "Noah's so determined to not be like his grandfather, that I'm worried he'll end up just like Alec."

A customer stepped up to the till, and I snapped my fingers at Tanya. I was in the middle of a meaningful conversation. She could do her job for once.

"From what I've heard, he's not anything like his grandfather, though I've never met the man."

"Alec wasn't always the way he is now."

"Why does that sound so ominous?"

Caroline smiled sadly. "He used to be driven. He had ideas. Lots of ideas. Loved making a business go."

I nodded, understanding her meaning. Noah had that same drive, too. I knew he thrived on the challenge of making a business profitable. It's why he couldn't walk away from the golf course. He felt that internal pressure to make it work. His worth was tied up in how well he did in business. I'd have to do something about that.

"When I married Alec, he thrived on a challenge the same as Noah. Then it became the challenge of starting something new. Always something new. Eventually, as time went on, he began looking for those challenges in other ways—if you know what I mean."

Yes, Noah had mentioned his grandfather's affairs. I nodded, not wanting to voice it out loud to Caroline.

"He didn't want to settle down. I raised our children, and he raised money—then spent it just as fast. When he no longer tried to keep those *things* a secret from me, I knew it was time to go. It wasn't a relationship I wanted to be modeled in front of our son and daughter."

"You two seem to be having a serious talk. I hope it's not about me," Cletus said as he stepped out from the back room. "I'm sorry I was late again, Caroline. That supplier was trying to raise delivery fees."

"Must be the same one Noah's been dealing with," I commented. Cletus glared at me.

"Am I paying you to stand here and talk?"

"I don't know, are you?"

He grumbled to himself while he filled a cup of coffee from the house coffee carafe. "One of these days, I'm going to fire you. I'm getting too old to deal with your attitude."

"And I'm too young to deal with yours."

"Children, please," Caroline cut in with a laugh. "We'll talk later, Page."

She patted my hand then followed Cletus to their regular table.

I was sure she was wrong. Noah was nothing like his grandfather. Sure, work had required a lot from him lately, but that would only be for a short season.

All he needed was help with the financial stress. He wouldn't turn into his grandfather, right?

Knocking on my parents' front door, I didn't wait for an answer before I opened it. I used knocking as a courtesy warning to my mother. She didn't like being surprised by finding me in the kitchen.

I stepped inside the house and shut the door quickly behind me, careful to not let the heat in.

"Mom! Where are you?"

"In the kitchen!" She called back. I stepped past the short entry hall and around the corner into the kitchen.

Baked goods covered every visible flat surface.

"Mom, what are you doing?"

She wiped her hands on her apron that said ~~Kiss~~ *Pay the Cook*, then walked over to plant a kiss on my cheek. "How are you, dear?" She hurried back to the mixer and shut it off.

"I'm good, Mom. What's all this?" Cupcakes, cookies, and pies lined the counter.

"Oh, the girls are part of a bake sale tomorrow for their dance team."

"Why aren't they in here helping?"

"They're over at a friend's this afternoon," she explained as she scooped out some frosting from the mixer and began spreading it on a chocolate cake.

Why was I not surprised? I headed to the sink and washed my hands.

"Mom, you're good at saving money." It was the understatement of the year. My mother could walk out of the grocery store with a prime rib for a dollar. Actually, she could probably get the grocery store to pay her to take it.

"I try." She frosted another cupcake and smoothed the icing on top.

"What would you do if you had a golf course that was failing financially?"

"Well, you can always cut costs. That's obvious." She set the cupcake plate on the island. "Or maybe they're not thinking outside of the box. Why, just the other day, I read about a man who was a golf ball diver."

"A what?" I scooped a finger full of frosting into my mouth.

"A golf ball diver. Each year, thousands of golf balls are lost on golf courses, often in the ponds. Golf ball divers dive to the bottom of the ponds and retrieve all the lost golf balls."

"How does picking up golf balls help with money?"

Mom gave me *the* look. The one where you wonder if she's about to disown you. "You sell them. The golf course sells used golf balls in the shops, or you can even resell them online. There's lots of money in golf balls."

"I wouldn't have thought of that. Thank you, Mom." I planted a kiss on her cheek and headed for the door.

"You're leaving so soon? You just got here!"

I stopped. She was right. I hadn't spent much time around the house since Noah, and I started dating. I took a few steps backward and snatched a cupcake. "Are you guys hanging around the house tonight? Noah's working tonight, so I don't know what to do with myself."

"Well, no, we actually have plans. The girls have a—"

I held up my hand. "Never mind."

"Dance recital." Mom finished. "Why don't you sit down and talk with me while you eat that cupcake? I want to know why you're asking about money and golf courses. Is it because of your new boyfriend?"

I sat down on the metal barstool and spent the next two hours talking about Noah with my mom while she baked enough goodies to feed the nations.

I still couldn't believe Alec Dunaway would leave his own grandson such a debt-ridden mess. If I ever met the man, I didn't think I could keep my mouth shut. I probably wouldn't even try.

Noah was having a great attitude about it and working his hardest to bring in new members. But that wouldn't immediately wipe away that debt. If he wanted to make a profit, he needed to get creative.

Thank goodness he had me to help him.

I'd made an entire list of ways for the golf course to bring in more money. Mom helped. If there were two things mom loved, it was pinching a penny and making a penny.

Today, I would be taking care of the first thing on my

list. Thanks to Mom, I knew a person could make a good living on diving for golf balls. The ponds were supposedly littered with golf balls that could be cleaned up and resold. It was like having money laying around in the water. When I first arrived at the golf course that morning, I'd asked Kent if anyone ever dived for them, and he said no. When I'd asked if he knew where Noah was, he said no. Kent had been as helpful as Tanya that morning.

When I asked Kent if things were tight financially, he said yes, and that Noah had been complaining about it earlier in the morning.

I peeled off my shirt and shorts then tossed them on top of my tennis shoes. I pulled the snorkel and mask from my backpack. Reaching in, I fished around until I found the laundry bag with a cinch top. I'd have to use it to hold the golf balls that I picked up.

Someone whistled at me. I turned around to see an older man with wispy hair waving in the breeze. He grinned at me and waved with his golf club—it almost toppled him over backward. He was approaching the seventh hole and looked like he should sit down and take a break at his age.

I reached into the bag one more time and grabbed a pair of flippers. I slipped them on my feet then rested the goggles on my head. I flopped toward the pond, readjusting my bikini straps as I went.

Operation golf ball retrieval was a go.

I put the snorkel in my mouth and lowered the goggles over my eyes.

"Page, wait!"

Noah's golf cart screeched to a halt a few feet away. Kent sat in the passenger seat, looking smug as ever. Noah jumped from the cart and hurried toward me. "What are you doing?"

He looked like he was fighting a grin as he took in my outfit. I'm sure if I saw myself, I'd be laughing too. It's not every day that a person is wearing snorkel gear on a golf course.

"I know this will sound strange—"

"You sound like you're in a tunnel."

I lifted my mask off my nose and eyes and rested it on my forehead. "I'm going diving for golf balls."

He looked at me, then at the pond, then at me again.

"No, you're not."

"Did you know you can resell them? If I bring up a few hundred golf balls, you could start reselling them in the clubhouse or even online. It could help solve some financial problems for you."

I watched as he started to scowl. He turned and pointed at Kent. "You told her about that?"

Kent shrugged. "She wanted to help."

"Don't blame Clark."

"Clark?" Noah asked.

"Kent. He loves my little name for him."

"I heard that!" Kent yelled from the cart.

"Back to the golf balls—I really want to help. You could wait here, and I'll bring you back the golf balls."

"Absolutely not. You think Lucifer is the only cottonmouth around here? How about any gators? You could get killed."

His voice was getting quieter and quieter as if it scared him to yell.

"Get in the golf cart." He glared at me and pointed to the cart.

I looked at where Kent was sitting in the passenger seat looking smug. I'm sure I'd love nothing more than to push him out of a speeding golf cart.

I flopped over to the driver's seat and sat down. I gave

Kent my most evil grin and rested my hands on the wheel, but then Noah was leaning into the golf cart. "Scoot over." With a sigh, I scooted over and made some room for him. It wasn't easy. Kent kept elbowing me in the side. There wasn't room for three people in the front of a golf cart.

Noah sat down, his leg brushing against mine. I was hyperaware of his presence since I was only wearing a bikini.

"Why don't you drive one of the golf carts with a back seat?"

"Kent gets car sick sitting in the back." He winked at me, and I knew I was forgiven. I didn't want him to be mad at me. Then again, it would be ridiculous if he was mad at me, especially since I only wanted to help him. I wasn't trying to sabotage his golf course—I was trying to save it.

I leaned closer to Noah, smelling his cinnamon gum. I could practically see the sparks radiating between us. I think I could sprawl across Kent and feel no different from lying on an uncomfortable air mattress. I felt nothing when his arm brush mine. Though it shouldn't have been a huge deal, every time Noah shifted or turned the cart, his body leaned a little closer to mine, making my heart speed up a little more each time.

Noah parked the cart and extended his hand to help me climb out of the cart—ever the gentleman.

"Sir! Sir!"

A middle-aged woman ran towards him. She was wearing a black button-up shirt with dark gray slacks. She wore a small black apron around her waist, and I recognized her as one of the waitresses that worked part-time.

"Sir, we have a problem in the kitchen." The woman spoke to him, but her eyes were on me, taking in my outfit.

Noah sighed. "I have a feeling I know what's going on. Kent will go with you and help. I'll be there soon."

Kent and the woman headed to the clubhouse, leaving Noah and me alone.

"What am I going to do with you, Page? Today's stunt could have got you killed!"

"It also could have helped with the finances," I mumbled. "No sense of adventure."

He narrowed his eyes at me. "Says the woman who lives in her parents' backyard."

I opened my mouth to tell him exactly where he could shove his opinions, but he cut me off.

"Let me tell you something, if it came down to finances or your life, I'd choose you every time."

I'd never melted into a puddle of happiness before. A puddle of embarrassment, sure. A puddle of sweat, definitely. But happiness? That was a puddle I'd gladly experience every day. It was incredibly frustrating when I still wanted to be mad at him for the comment about living in my parents' yard.

"What if—"

"No more ideas. I can't handle anymore of them."

"What if I just—"

He leaned a fraction of an inch closer. I loved pushing his buttons and finding out exactly how far his restraint went. I had yet to see it snap in any way. I'd seen him wrestle himself over it, but he always won—from the way he schooled his expressions to always saying the right thing. He never let himself go.

"Coffee tonight? And you can tell me about your idea then?"

I smiled and nodded.

"Café du Monde?"

"Yes, please."

He smiled, then headed towards the restaurant.

The afternoon couldn't come fast enough.

I finished the last touches to my eyelashes just as there was a knock on my front door. I grabbed my lip stain and swiped another layer on. I didn't want to be the girl to leave lipstick stuck to Noah's lips at the end of the Café du Monde date. I was respectful like that—lip stain all the way.

I walked out of my small bathroom, past my bed covered with boxes, and squeezed between easels draped with fabric. I opened the door to find Noah standing on my step.

It's not that I expected to find someone else there, but it didn't take away from the effect of finding such a handsome man standing on my front step waiting for me. He wore dark wash jeans and a short-sleeve shirt; his usual Ivy League hair tussled. His woody cologne mixed nicely with the ever-present cinnamon smell that followed him.

"You look beautiful." He smiled, and it made it worth every painstaking eyelash I'd glued on. He looked good casual. In our whole time of dating, I had never seen him wear jeans. It was a good look on him.

While he'd dressed down for our date, I'd dressed up and put on a pale green dress along with a set of white heels. I had white, crocheted earrings and a white belt.

"You look good. I think I like you in casual clothes. You're more approachable."

He frowned. "You mean, I seemed unapproachable before?"

I grabbed my purse and stepped out the door. I grabbed his hand before I answered him. "You were intimidating until I realized you were a big softy underneath."

He squeezed my hand gently as we walked down the path together. "I'll have to practice a little harder. I'd like to think I could intimidate someone."

I shook my head, "You're too nice. The only people you're going to scare are people like me who want to go golf cart sledding."

He raised an eyebrow at me. "If I ever catch you golf cart sledding..."

I laughed and leaned around to tap his chest. "Don't make threats you don't plan on carrying out."

He wrapped his arm around my waist and pulled me to him. He said nothing, just leaned down and kissed me. "See, I don't make empty threats."

"That threat won't work—I like it too much."

He smiled down at me. "Let's find some beignets."

"Sounds good to me." We walked through the gate that led to the front yard and were greeted to the sight of Jenny and Mack climbing out of Jenny's car. They had parked at the end of my parents' drive, blocking off the mailbox.

"Hey!" Jenny yelled. Did she have any other volume other than loud? Probably not. She was wearing her usual outfit of t-shirt and jean shorts. Her curly hair hung around her shoulders, and she wasn't wearing a stitch of makeup. It would have horrified my mother, but

I always thought Jenny was beautiful without it. She had a forever young face. Even though she was only two years younger than me, people assumed she was still in high school.

She hadn't sent me a text to say she was stopping by— at least I didn't think so. "What are you guys doing here?"

"We were coming to steal you for a night out."

Usually, I loved it when Jenny stopped by to hang out. Usually Mack came with her, and we always had a blast. But I wanted Noah to myself. I wanted to spend time with him without us being at the golf course, or in the coffee shop, or hanging out with Cameron. I didn't want to share him—no matter how much I loved spending time with Jenny.

"We already have plans, thanks, though."

"Where are you guys going?"

"Café du Monde."

"Perfect! We'll follow you there!" Jenny jumped back in the car and motioned for Mack to climb in again. Mack shrugged and mouthed "sorry" to us.

I glanced up at Noah when he opened my door for me. "How are your evasive driving skills?"

"We're about to find out," he answered drily, and I climbed into the car.

"Have you met Jenny yet?"

"She came golfing with Mack and your aunt and uncle yesterday. She leaves an impression."

I lifted my hands in the air. "Preach."

He chuckled.

"Actually, she's a lot of fun—only a little different than most people are used to."

An hour later and we were walking down the riverfront towards Café du Monde. Somehow, Noah had managed to lose sight of Mack and Jenny. I don't know how since he drove the speed limit—something anyone in the Boone family was incapable of.

Unfortunately, when we walked up to Café du Monde, Mack and Jenny had already saved a table, and Jenny was standing up in the crowded space whistling for us.

"Do you suppose there's a chance we're not blood-related?" I asked. Noah shook his head and guided me through the maze of tables to where they sat with three plates of beignets.

"What took you so long?" Jenny asked when we sat down.

"He drives like a grandpa."

Noah gave me a mock glare, then leaned closer to whisper, "Keep going and see where it gets you."

I shivered and fought a smile.

"I can't remember the last time I've played tourist," Mack said as he picked up a beignet. A soft breeze blew through the open-air cafe, blowing a puff of powdered sugar off the beignet and into Noah's face. I reached up and brushed it off, thinking I'd prefer to kiss it off.

"So… Jenny has some news." Mack said, clearing his throat. I straightened back up, but not before I caught the twinkle in Noah's eye.

I turned my attention to Jenny. I'd been so focused on Noah, enjoying my time with him that I hadn't stopped to consider that maybe Jenny needed me for something.

"What is it, Jenny?"

Jenny smiled nervously—very unlike Jenny—then shoved an entire beignet into her mouth—very much like Jenny.

I flattened my hand on the table-top and looked at her expectantly. When she reached for another beignet to keep her mouth occupied, I snatched it out of her reach.

"Spill or I'll eat the last one."

She looked down at the table and mumbled something.

I kicked her—gently—under the table. "You know you can tell me anything, right?"

She brushed the powdered sugar into a neat little pile. "Of course. But I know you'll be mad about this."

"I never get mad," I scoffed. Mack snorted and Noah coughed.

She finally met my eyes, and her eyes looked steely. "I'm moving to Oregon."

I gasped and inhaled a little powdered sugar from the beignet in my hand. It caused me to go into a coughing fit with Noah gently patting my back.

"You okay?" He asked.

I nodded but didn't take my eyes off Jenny. "What are you talking about?"

She shrugged as if moving over two thousand miles away wasn't a big deal. "I'm going to stay with Uncle Presley there."

"No! Not the Oregon Boones."

"Yup. The Oregon Boones."

"Have you gone insane?"

"I'm going insane doing the same things over and over again. I need a change."

I shook my head. "I've never been to Oregon. How are you going to get around when you're there?"

She snorted, "Believe it or not, Oregon has paved roads just like Louisiana."

"That's debatable. I've heard stories from Mom and Dad about Oregon. None of it was good."

Noah glanced back and forth between us.

Mack picked up his cup of coffee and leaned back in his chair as he explained to Noah, "The Oregon Boones are a special brand of crazy. They've basically become a legend. They're the threat our parents used to use to scare us kids into behaving."

"Why is that?" Noah asked as he took a sip from his water bottle.

"They live in rural Oregon. I don't know if it's even really a town. Supposedly they have an ongoing feud with another family. There isn't even a real bridge that crosses the creek. The Oregon Boones are the kind that drive around with shotguns across their laps. We've heard that it's like taking a step back in time when you go to Boones-Dock."

"Boones-Dock?"

Mack smiled, but I wasn't finding any of this funny. "That's the name of their little town."

Noah shook his head and looked amused. "Sounds interesting. You sure you want to go there, Jenny?"

Jenny shrugged. "I guess I'll find out for myself. It'll be fun to see firsthand."

I slammed back into my chair. Stunned. Mad. Sad. Jealous. "That, wow, that's great."

Jenny nodded as she folded her arms across her chest. "I can tell you're excited about it."

I shook my head. "I want to be excited for you."

Jenny's face softened. "I know. You can always come visit me."

If I was honest with myself, I wasn't excited for her. We were supposed to go together. She didn't even talk to me about her plans to go. She'd confided in Mack—which was horrible. Everyone confided in Mack. He was always the first to know. "I'll probably have to bring you basic living supplies—like toilet paper and sanity."

Jenny narrowed her eyes and leaned towards me. "Or maybe I'll get to broaden my horizons. Did you think of that? Instead of just talking about moving somewhere new and doing something different, I'm going out and doing it." Jenny stood up and waved for Mack to follow. "Come on, Mack. Let's go."

Mack stood reluctantly. "Sorry, Page. I should have warned you. She's been a little touchy about it. She'll come around."

With a wave to Noah, he took off after Jenny, who was weaving past a few street performers.

I slammed my elbow on the table and rested my chin in my hand. "She's leaving me."

"I'm sorry." Noah rested an arm around the back of my chair and angled himself toward me. "I know you're close with your cousins."

"It's not just that. It's all so selfish. We'd planned on going to Portland together. We'd planned on visiting Boones-Dock together. It's selfish of her."

Noah took a sip of his water as he watched me with his steady gaze.

I slumped forward. "Okay, fine. It's selfish of me to want her to plan her life around me. I'm the selfish one, but I'm still mad."

"You're the least selfish person I know."

I leaned my head against his shoulder despite the humid heat. "It's only that—well, we talked about traveling ever since we were little girls. We'd planned to do it together. She's the one I go on weekend trips with. I've been saving for our big trips, but we haven't done anything. Nothing big. Not like we'd planned as little girls."

He reached up and gently brushed his fingers against my shoulder.

"Now she's going without me. I'll still be here. I know I should be happy she's doing something. And goodness knows she needs a break from her family."

"Come on. You can tell me all about your travel plans

you made with Jenny while we play tourist. I'd love to hear about them." I smiled as he gently pulled me to my feet and made our way outside the Café.

"I'm sorry I'm such a grump," I apologized.

"It's okay." He squeezed my hand as we walked towards St. Louis Cathedral. The street artists lined the road. The jazz music filled the air. And I still felt lost at sea.

"We were supposed to travel the world together—live in exotic places—and she's doing it without me."

"I don't know if I'd call Oregon exotic."

I waved a hand through the air. "She's still going somewhere."

"Why don't you go?"

I glanced at him, wondering if he'd lost his mind. "For example, money seems to be a major issue. What I want to do and what makes money are two different things."

"And what is it you want to do?"

"I love creating things. I love drawing, designing, painting."

His lips twitched, but he nodded. "Why can't you have a career in those things?"

"Because I didn't like working in an art gallery. It's just not my thing. I'd rather be creating something—like this art and wine night that I'm planning for you. I can't remember the last time I've had this much fun working on a project."

"Maybe that's your answer."

"What, being the official art and wine night coordinator?"

He smiled and squeezed my hand. "Find the part of it you like and find out how you can turn it into a career. I believe you could make a career out of anything you put your mind to. It doesn't have to be one thing, either."

"I'd be tied down here. I'd be stuck here with a career."

He looked at me with raised eyebrows, a challenge in his eye. "Is that all that's holding you back from pursuing something you love?"

I swallowed the lump in my throat and looked straight ahead. It was annoying how he saw straight through me. "Fine. It's just that I've dreamed and planned my trips for so long, what if I travel and it's still not the answer? What if I go around the world, and I'm bored? What's next after that? I get bored so easy. I hate doing the same thing over and over again."

"Traveling isn't going to make you bored. It's also not going to be the answer to whatever it is you're looking for."

"I know," I whispered. "That's why I'm scared. I've acted like traveling will solve all my problems, but if I travel the world, I'm still bringing myself."

Noah released my hand and wrapped an arm around my shoulders. "Why would you want to run from yourself?"

Stopping in the middle of the sidewalk, I turned to face him. "I'm indecisive. I never finished college. I'm still not sure what to do with my life. The one person I could count on to be at the same stage as me, was Jenny. Now she's moving. I'll still be working in the coffee shop when my sisters and little brother are doctors, lawyers, or whatnot. I'll still be dreaming about traveling, never doing it, and working part-time jobs to make ends meet. What kind of person am I?"

Noah pulled me into his chest and hugged me. "The best kind. No one's life looks the same. Stop comparing your life with other people's. It doesn't have to look the same. Who told you that you needed to change?"

I let myself sink into the warmth of his arms. It was sweltering hot already, and I knew I was sweating leaning on him, but it was worth it.

"Why are you so good to me all the time?"

He chuckled, causing his chest to shake under my cheek. "Because you keep sending me animals."

"I knew there was an ulterior motive," I laughed.

"Come on. Let's go inside the cathedral and take an annoying number of selfies. Then afterward, we'll go walk the streets and let people hustle us out of our money."

I nodded. "That sounds amazing."

Chapter Sixteen

NOAH

It took Page a full two days to come around to supporting Jenny in her decision to move to Oregon. She'd explained to me that Jenny didn't have the most supportive family and that it would be good for her to put some distance between them.

Page spent one of our dates telling me about all the activities she'd found for Jenny to do when she moved to Oregon. Numbered at the top was snowboarding in the winter and visiting a natural hot spring. Page thought the hot springs sounded fantastic. She told me we should fly out to Oregon to go with Jenny—I told her I didn't want to see a bunch of naked people. She agreed that that part didn't sound great either.

She had finally showed me her ideas for the art and wine night. It would be hard to know if it would be successful until after the art night. We weren't requiring RSVP's and were instead making it open to the public. Page was working out a deal with the art gallery owner, Carlotta, and was doing a big favor for me. I was a little nervous to see how the decorations turned out. Page made me promise that she would have free rein. I agreed and regretted it whenever I remembered Edwina and Zeke.

I took a sip of my Coke as I watched my sister across the table from me. We'd finally managed to get lunch together, and it had been far too long.

"How are you? Really?" Dani asked as she shoveled food into her mouth faster than someone at a hot dog eating contest.

"Um, I'm fine."

More salad disappeared.

"Are you okay?"

"Yeah! Great! Just great," she answered between gulps of water and bites of food.

"Dani, why don't you take a breath between those bites? It's your day off. The kids are with mom. You're not on call."

She dropped her fork with a clatter, and her shoulders drooped. "I hadn't even realized what I was doing. I'm so used to having to rush if I want to eat a meal."

"Are you sure that's healthy?"

"Who's the pediatrician here?" she asked with raised eyebrows. Then she smiled and gestured to the salad left in front of her. "I try to make healthy choices for my speed eating."

"Why do you feel so stressed?"

She sighed as she took a long—slow—sip of water. "You know, I'm actually really happy right now. I think it's more from habit. Lunch is always rushed at work because of over-scheduling appointments. Then when I'm home, I'm taking care of the kids."

"You need a vacation."

"Yes, we're planning a trip to Disney Land with the kids—"

I shook my head. "No, Dani, you and Robby need to

take a trip. Just the two of you. Go find a beach somewhere and lay on it."

Her eyes narrowed. "This coming from my workaholic brother? Mr. Thrives-on-business?"

She wasn't wrong, but everyone has a breaking point, and she looked like she was getting close to hers. "Sell your mini-farm."

Her horrified look made me think I'd accidentally suggested that she sell one of her children. "My children will grow up in the country. They'll get to have pets. Don't ever suggest such a horrible thing!"

"Noted. How are Edwina and Zeke doing?"

"Sydney carries 'Wina' with her everywhere. I even caught her smuggling that chicken into her bed. Remind me to pay you back someday. How did they end up at the golf course? You never told me."

That didn't sound so good. I didn't want her to pay me back—and I wasn't sure how to tell her about where the animals came from.

Dani and I hadn't talked in a couple of months. With her work and mine, we were like ships passing in the night. Getting a kid-free lunch with her? Pretty much a pumpkin spice miracle. Needless to say, she would not be happy with me when she found out I was dating someone and hadn't told her.

"My girlfriend gave them to me."

The bite of lettuce on Dani's fork fell onto her lap. She didn't notice. "Girlfriend? Mom didn't tell me! Neither did Grandma."

"I know. I'm sorry. I wanted to be the one to tell you. And it's just that work has been crazy, and whenever I take time off, Page and I spend time together."

"Oh."

I nodded. Dani knew that I wouldn't take time away

from work unless it was a woman I was serious about. Once upon a time, I'd told Dani I wouldn't take time off work for a girl unless I planned to marry her.

"Oh, I see." She nodded and dabbed at her mouth with a napkin. "What does the ring look like?"

She'd remembered—and knew I would already have a ring in mind.

"I've decided on a rose gold design with a brown diamond. It's not finished yet."

She nodded. Dani was fantastic. I didn't have to explain myself to her—she understood. "When do I get to meet her?"

"She has a strange schedule."

"What does she do?"

"She's an artist who used to work in an art gallery."

"How prestigious."

I chuckled. "It's not that kind of art gallery—she quit a couple last week."

"Okay, now you're just making me curious."

"But she's a barista—or coffee shop owner—in the mornings and a wandering soul with a love for painting and decorating."

"Wow. You actually know this girl. This is real."

I fought the urge to shrug. "It feels real to me. I only hope that I'm enough for her."

Dani's gaze sharpened on me. "What do you mean?"

"She's fun. She's exciting. She's not afraid to live outside of the box."

"Aha. Well, maybe you level each other out. Has she gotten you to do anything you normally wouldn't?"

"I'm supposed to go to a Harvest party at her family's this week."

"What? That is super serious. You're meeting the family."

"Yeah, I guess so. I've already met her immediate family and two of her cousins, Mack and Jenny. Going to the Halloween party isn't that big of a deal."

"You hate Halloween."

"I don't hate it, per se. I just don't care about it."

"Even worse. You're apathetic about a holiday, and now she's got you going to a Harvest party meeting the family. The kids don't understand why you don't love the candy."

"Three-hundred-sixty-four days out of the year, parents teach their kids to not talk to strangers. Then one day a year, they tell them to knock on strangers' doors and ask for candy. And you think I'm messed up for not liking Halloween." I shook my head. I had perfectly good reasons for not liking Halloween.

She laughed, "I can't wait to meet the girl who talked you into Halloween. What's she like?"

"She's—well, she's the only woman I've met that's like her. She throws herself into everything. She doesn't hold back."

"Not reserved? How refreshing." Dani leaned forward to steal a drink of Coke from my glass.

"I know, right? She's not afraid to say how she feels. She doesn't pretend to be something she's not. I don't have to pretend with her either. I can just be myself."

Dani glanced at me sharply. "Does she know how you feel?"

"I've told her."

"You've told her? Hmm." She took another long drink of my Coke.

"What do you mean by that? You know I wouldn't say something unless I meant it."

"Of course, I know that. But I've also had the benefit of knowing you your whole life. She hasn't." She finally set my glass back on the table. "You're not as, well, shall we say, effusive as some people. I'm glad you've told her how you feel."

It was a good thing I knew that Page understood me. She knew that I cared more for her than anything else. I knew she cared for me too. I just didn't know if I could compare with the rest the world had to offer.

"Let me tell you about the art night Page is planning for the golf course..."

Chapter Seventeen

PAGE

oah sat with me in my tiny house while I did something so rare, so out of character, I needed someone there to witness the event so they could tell the tale to future generations.

I was folding my laundry.

Noah had taken the afternoon off—also a rare event. He didn't know that I silenced his phone while he was in the bathroom. I didn't need Kent calling and ruining this perfect afternoon for me. Kent could handle any problems that arose at the golf course—I was going to enjoy Noah's company.

I already knew how I was going to set up the art night. Noah was taking care of the extra staff, and I was taking care of the displays and decorations. It was the most fun I'd had doing a job. It was something I could happily do every day.

Now it was just a matter of figuring out how.

"If I'm going to your family's Halloween party, I'm going to need an outfit."

I couldn't believe he was coming to the Halloween

party. For one, it was much too soon for him to meet Mimi. I didn't want him to meet several of the Boone family members—ever. I was too scared he wouldn't want to stick around after that.

"Are you sure? Because my family likes to go all out for holidays. There's even going to be a pumpkin carving contest. I mean, if you're not up for it..."

He slid the rolling chair away from my desk and towards me. He stopped when it hit my Sherpa rug. "Oh, I'm up for it. Don't think I can't handle a little family get-together. Besides, I'm looking forward to meeting Mimi."

I tapped a finger to my lips. "Really, it might be too much for your sensitive—"

I didn't get to finish. His large hand shot out and latched onto my knee and squeezed, making me yelp with laughter. His other hand reached out and grasped my other knee, squeezing while I gasped for air.

"Now who's sensitive?" He grinned.

"Mercy!" I grasped his wrists, and he stopped tickling my knees. "Okay. You're not sensitive. But we better go shopping for an outfit for you. We take our costume competition seriously."

"I'm not surprised." He stood up and pulled me with him. "Where do we go shopping for a Halloween costume? I've never been."

I stopped at the threshold. "You've never been shopping for a Halloween costume? Who are you?"

"I'm your boyfriend." He smiled, and I couldn't help but smile back because I liked the sound of that.

But there was an important question I needed answered. "Why haven't you been shopping for a costume?"

He smirked. "I haven't dressed up for Halloween since I was eight. You were wrong about me planning to be

Captain America when you were guessing the first day we met."

I gaped at him. "This is—wow. This is horrific. You've never been shopping for a costume as an adult. This is the saddest thing I've ever heard."

I swiped at a few fake tears and patted his back. "Come on. This will be an experience you'll never forget. I feel like I'm back to being your fairy godmother."

"Anything I do with you is unforgettable," he answered as he followed me out the door.

I grabbed my keys out of my clutch and headed toward my car, except he grabbed my elbow and gently steered me towards his car. "I'll drive."

"Okay, Sunday driver." I climbed into the passenger seat and inhaled the leather and cinnamon smell. "What is with you and cinnamon gum? You eat it like it's going out of style."

"You sure you want to know?" He asked as he turned onto the highway.

"What—does chewing it give you superpowers? Are your good looks derived from chewing cinnamon gum? If you stop chewing it do you age fifty years?"

He chuckled as he grabbed a piece out of the middle console and popped it in his mouth. "Nope. Even worse. I quit smoking."

I stared at him. "You smoked?"

He nodded but kept his eyes on the road.

"Wow. I never would have imagined you as someone who smoked. Isn't it common knowledge that it will kill you? How often?"

"I'm not sure how often people die from it."

I leaned over and smacked his arm.

He grimaced. "Two packs a day."

I reached into the middle console and unwrapped a

second piece of gum and handed it to him. He laughed. "I've gotten past it—mostly. Now the gum has become a habit. But when I talk about smoking or smell it, sometimes it makes those old cravings come back. More than anything, it was my way of de-stressing."

"Walking through the French Quarter must be pure torture for you."

"It's not so bad. It's more like it's a combination of stressors. I took up the habit when I was in business school. I can't even blame it on poor high school choices. A friend of mine was diagnosed with lung cancer a few years ago. It was the wake-up call I needed. So… I threw out all my packs. I think the cinnamon gum might be a harder habit to break now."

I reached over and laced my fingers through his and held tight. "You're a strong man; you know that? Quitting smoking. I've tried to quit coffee before, and it only lasted a day. Had the worst migraine of my life. I think I went into a rage. It wasn't pretty."

"It's easy to picture you in a rage."

"How rude!" Leaning over, I smacked his chest, and he merely raised his eyebrows. He exaggeratedly rubbed his chest where I hit him.

"Where are we going? Where do people shop for a Halloween costume?"

"At the Halloween store, of course."

He nodded seriously. "Of course. I should have known. The Halloween store."

He turned and gave me a "yeah right" look.

"Seriously. That's where we're going," I told him.

"You're joking. There's such a thing as a Halloween store?"

I laughed. "Of course! It's in Lampton. It's a seasonal store. Kylie's mom, Rose, used to drive us every year. Right now, it's filled with Halloween merchandise. At Christmas time, it will be full of Christmas stuff."

"What about summer-time?"

"I think it's only open like six months out of the year. Besides, there are a million other stores around that sell summer things."

"I don't know if I'll believe you until I see it."

Forty minutes later, we were walking into the giant Halloween store in Lampton.

"Okay. I believe you," he said with a laugh as a little girl dressed like a princess skipped out of the store, holding her mom's hand.

He opened the door for me, and we stepped into a whirlwind of Halloween decorations: flashing green and purple lights, ghosts flying through the rafters. A fog machine filled up the entryway.

"My eyes are burning," he complained.

"Oh, be quiet. It's not that bad."

The swirling lights and screeches from flying ghosts were the quintessential Halloween decor. The over-whelming smell of plastic textiles filled the store. Little children chased each other up and down the aisles wearing masks while their parents ran after them.

We walked up and down the aisles taking in everything. Noah kept making outfit suggestions, and I kept telling him no. He picked up a minuscule police officer outfit; he looked at me with raised eyebrows and pointed at the mini skirt with handcuffs hanging from it.

I laughed and made him put it back. He blushed as he did it.

We continued walking the aisles until we reached the superhero section. He grinned and winked at me as he reached for something.

I slapped his hand away from the shield. "You are not going as Captain America."

"Why not? Besides, maybe I'll go as what I want to go as."

I took a step towards him and slammed my hands on my hips. "Are you arguing with me?"

He shoved his hands in his pockets and grinned. "Yes."

I leaned forward and placed a hand on his chest. "You won't win."

He winked. "Maybe you'll get used to losing with me around."

"I'll take that as a challenge." I stood on my tiptoes and at first only pressed my lips against his. Then I gently tugged at his bottom lip with my teeth. A ragged breath left him as I pulled away.

Patting his chest once more, I pretended like it didn't make my heart beat irregularly when I kissed him.

"We're going as Danny Zuko and Sandy. It's a must."

"Who's Danny Zuko?"

It was going to be a long and delightful afternoon of Halloween shopping and informing Noah about Danny Zuko.

"Don't think I don't notice that Captain America pin on your lapel."

The sneak grinned, clearly proud of his rebellion. We'd survived Halloween shopping, and three days later we were at Mimi's property in the country. The entire Boone family was there, and Noah had been overloaded with introductions.

"You can't get your way in everything, Page."

"But...I could try."

He laughed. "No, you already try."

"It's annoying when people don't do what I want. First Jenny, now you. Pretty soon, the whole world is going to ignore me."

He shrugged. "Regular old anarchy under the Page regime."

I sighed. "Do you think I'm too pushy?"

He picked up his glass and took a big sip. When I started to worry he would drown, I pulled it out of his hands. "You can't hide behind that all night. I'm pushy, aren't I?"

He shook his head, "No. I don't think "pushy" is the right word. You're full of life, and everything you do is with energy and purpose. The way you make a cup of coffee in the mornings. The way you give your tippers your most winning smile—"

"How did you—"

"Yes, I noticed your smile technique at the coffee shop." He smiled at me. "When you do something, you throw your whole self into it. If you have been pushy, it hasn't been maliciously."

I opened my mouth to answer him, but he interrupted me as he stepped closer. "Don't look now, but a walking fruit tree coming our way," Noah whispered in my ear. His warm breath drifted across my cheek. The soft leather jacket he was wearing brushed against my bare shoulder. I was wearing so much hairspray that I could see the fruit tree walking through a haze.

"Page, honey. You're in trouble."

I spun around and faced the one and only Mimi.

"Hi Mimi."

She scowled at me. "Is that how you greet your grandmother? Where's my hug?"

I pointed to her dress that looked like an imitation of a fruit platter. "I don't think I can reach you past all the apples and oranges."

Her face softened. "Good point. I don't want to knock any of this off. Did you know it's all real? Do you think I'll stand a chance of winning?"

"You look amazing, ma'am. I'm sure you'll win." Noah assured her.

"She'll win," I added. "She's the biggest cheat this family has."

Mimi plucked a grape off her dress and tossed it at me. "I appear before the same judges you do."

"Pops is partial! Especially since you make his breakfast."

"Are you accusing me of accepting bribes?"

I spun around to find my grandpa—Pops—standing beside Noah.

His thinning white hair was combed over to the side, but his fluffy beard made up for the lack of hair on top.

I planted a kiss on his weather cheek. "Hi Pops. You haven't met my boyfriend yet. This is Noah."

Pops studied my face for a moment before he turned to shake Noah's hand.

"Good luck." He glanced at Mimi and winked.

"Good luck with what?" Noah asked.

"Well, Page is a little unconventional. No one can put up with her for long." Mimi said.

Noah's eyes narrowed as he glared at Mimi, unaware of the test she was putting to him. "Then everyone else is missing out."

Mimi's face broke into a big smile. "I knew I liked you from the first time I saw you. Same as that Hagen boy."

Noah chuckled at her glee. "Do I pass the test?"

"Most definitely."

He rubbed a hand against his jaw as he asked, "Exactly how far ahead of Hagen am I?"

I poked him in the chest. "Leave poor defenseless Hagen out of this."

"I'm not poor and defenseless!" Hagen yelled from across the yard. He was sitting at one of the picnic tables he'd built. Kylie and Mack sat next to him.

Even with all of the younger kids running around the tables and yelling, it hadn't deafened my loud voice. Jenny was rubbing off on me. I'd forgotten how much sound carried at Pops and Mimi's property along the river.

"That's right! You're not poor and defenseless. Just defenseless!" Noah called back to him with a grin.

Mimi's loud laugh rose above the rest of the noise in the yard. "Oh, I like you a lot. It's good to be competitive in this family."

Mimi grabbed Noah's hand and mine then dragged us after her toward the podium. "Almost time to judge the costumes."

Noah leaned down and whispered in my ear, "If we lose, it's because I didn't dress myself."

Chapter Eighteen
NOAH

*W*e lost the costume competition on Halloween. Mimi won, and Pops had an exceptionally guilty look on his face. Page was right; there was something crooked going on there.

For the next ten days after Halloween, I took Page out on as many dates as possible, experiencing everything New Orleans had to offer in between work and prepping for the art night.

She was incredible.

We stood outside the dining area at the clubhouse. Page hadn't allowed me in there while she organized a team of decorators and event staff. Considering it was my business that she was taking over, I should have found it in me to care. But despite her earlier attempts at marketing with a petting zoo, I really hoped she could pull off an art display. I'd seen what she did in the art gallery—and it looked great.

She was practically jumping up and down in front of me with excitement. I watched as she reached into my jacket pocket and searched around. I'd never had anyone search my coat pockets before—especially not while I was wearing it.

"What are you doing?"

She ignored me and checked my breast pocket.

"Aha! I knew you had some with you."

She waved my pack of gum in front of my nose.

"How did you know that was there?"

"I could smell it."

She unwrapped a piece and popped it in her mouth, then carefully tucked the pack of gum back into my pocket. "And now I know why. It's my favorite kind." She smiled and began chewing the gum. "Come on. I'll show you what I'm working on."

"You know Page, a friend of mine recommended a great event planner if this is too much—"

"I've got this." She promised and then she grabbed my hand and tugged me through the double doors that led to the large room. Due to past history, I had a moment of panic—wondering how she had chosen to decorate. What I saw astounded me. She'd transformed the entire dining hall. The tables lined the outside of the room while the art was displayed throughout the center of the room. There were three long tables in the center of the room.

The dark green and pastel colors complimented each other while the mahogany accents set off the rest of the room.

A conglomeration of art pieces was stacked together to spell out The Garden in a six-foot-tall display.

"Wow, Page... this is..."

Her face fell. "I knew I should have gone with the chartreuse and charcoal."

"No." I looked around again. "Page, this is amazing! You've transformed this place. It's incredible."

Her eyes widened, and she stared at me. "You think so?"

"Yes, I really think so. This." I gestured to the room. "This is what we've needed for the golf course."

"I didn't know if the color theme was right or not."

Out of everything going on in the room, she was worried about the color theme. What she wasn't worried about was the themed tables and art displays around the serving tables. It was set up in a way that any way a person went to get to the food tables, they had to walk through a display and encourage bidding.

The bidding pieces were set up at the standing tables, and other pieces hung from the ceiling.

"Page, I don't know what to say."

"Try "you're fired." Maybe 'blacklisted.'"

I pivoted to face her, shoving my hands in my pockets. "Try "you're hired." It looks fantastic."

I barely had time to pull my hands back out of my pockets in time to catch her when she flew at me. She wrapped her arms around my neck and her legs around my waist, clinging to me like a spider monkey. "You like it!" she exclaimed.

"I hope I'm the only one who gets hugged like this by you."

"Yup. You are. Well, maybe Kylie. But last time I did this, she dropped me."

I wrapped my arms around her and walked to the center of the room, still carrying her. "This is going to be a hit. I can feel it."

She leaned back far enough to grin at me. "I'm so glad you like it."

"I'm serious. I will gladly hire you to be an event coordinator here."

She shook her head. "No, I don't think that's a good

idea. But I would love to help if you decide to keep doing these events."

She slid back down to her feet. She walked over to the table and pulled two water bottles out of a large bag. She handed me one, then held the other up in the air. "Here's to the first art night at The Garden!"

She tapped her water bottle to mine then took a sip. I smiled at her and followed suit. If an event like this were a regular thing, my golf course could turn around even faster than I projected.

The art night was a roaring success. We gained more members, booked two weddings, and had raving reviews about our new chef and menu. There were demands for more art nights.

It turned out so well that we did another. And another. And then it turned into a twice-monthly event.

I was busier than ever at the course, and Page was phenomenal, helping orchestrate all the art nights. She was toying with the idea of doing design—seasonal décor for businesses. She decorated The Garden for Christmas and a few business owners I knew asked about my decorator.

Page was busy looking into the logistics of starting a business like that. I'd offered to help her with the legalities and tax part of her business, but I didn't want to crowd her. She was moving forward with her life—deciding what she wanted. I didn't want to add unnecessary pressure, so I'd backed off while she worked out the particulars.

It felt as though we had settled into our relationship. I was falling for her hard—no, I'd already fallen. I was there. I wanted to spend the rest of my life with her, and now I kept a ring on me at all times to remind myself why I was working so hard at the golf course right now.

The only problem we faced was how busy I was at the golf course. I didn't have as much time as I wanted to spend it with Page.

She was so understanding. Every man should find himself a woman as understanding as Page. I planned on spending the rest of my life with her. I only hoped she felt the same way. Once everything was finished at the golf course, Kent would step up as manager, and I would be free to find another business to buy and run. Hopefully something less time consuming. Maybe I would focus on expanding my coffee shop chain.

I knocked on Page's door—it was seven o'clock, our regular date time on a Sunday. She opened the door and leapt into my arms. It was beginning to be a habit—one I hoped she never quit.

"Want to see what I've been working on today?"

I nodded and followed her into the small cottage. There were poster boards everywhere covered with pictures. There was a large sign painted Front Page Seasonal Decor.

"I'm not sure about the name yet, but I guess it will

have to do because I already created a website and social media pages. I've started running local ads as of an hour ago and been working on cross-promotion on local pages. So far, I've been booked to decorate for a birthday party and a graduation party. I used some pictures from the art gallery events. Lottie already wrote me a review from my work at the gallery. She is a gem for not being upset at my quitting."

"You did all of this in a day?"

She shrugged. "It was my day off. I decided you were right. The only thing standing in my way was me. If I wanted to do something I enjoy, I'm going to have to take a risk. Now we'll see if I can make this into a full-time job or not."

I shook my head as she sat down at the laptop and pulled up a website. She was starting a business on a fly by the seat of her pants decision. If that wasn't the most Page-like thing I'd ever seen, I didn't know what was.

"Your website looks great. Who did you hire to do it?"

She shook her head. "I just spent some time reading how-to blogs this morning and figured it out myself. Wasn't too hard. I've already grown my mailing list to a hundred people."

Running a hand over my face, I sat down next to her so she could show me her site. We skipped going to dinner and instead ordered pizza while she showed me exactly how much she could get done in fifteen hours. I decided she could take over the world in about a week if she put her mind to it.

Chapter Nineteen

PAGE

We were on our seventh art night. I couldn't be happier about the success Noah was having. Unfortunately, with that success he was busier than ever. He'd recently discovered that his grandfather had bribed two of the kitchen staff to sabotage some things. What a lovely family to be in. What a bitter old man that was desperate to see everyone else miserable around him!

I'd never met the man, and now I never wanted to.

Noah was mingling with some guests while I stood at the center table, loading up a plate of shrimp. I'd worked an early shift at the coffee shop that morning, then went to The Garden to finish setting up for the art night.

I grabbed two more shrimp because I needed sustenance.

"Who are you?" An older gentleman with bushy eyebrows barked at me.

"I'm Page," I shot back.

"What are you doing here?"

"Eating appetizers."

He looked at me with a snarl. "I mean, what are you doing here with my grandson. You're not the woman he needs at his side."

"Hmm, and you figured that out in thirty seconds, how?" I really didn't like this guy. Even more so once I realized why I recognized him. He was Noah's grandfather. There was no way I could pretend to be nice to such a big jerk. I didn't even try.

"You're too colorful."

I glanced down at my cream dress and matching shoes. I ran my hand through my hair, straightening out the big tangle curls. "I know my hair's a little browner than usual, I'll have to switch back to my old stylist. That way, we can make sure we cater to your every whim."

"So, you're a smart one too. You'd be horrible at reeling in potential members."

"And you're comparing me to your track record?"

He straightened up. "Why, yes, I am."

I laughed. I knew I was colorful. That was me, and I didn't intend to change for anyone—Noah had helped reiterate that to me when I doubted myself.

"You're laughing at me?" The old man's forehead was turning an unnatural shade of red.

"Let me get this straight. You left a debt-ridden golf course to your grandson, and you're telling me I can't bring in new business? It sounds like you and I should get along fine since you didn't bring in any business, either."

His face smoothed out, and his voice quieted. "Look around you. These are the upstanding business members of the community. Do you think that they are going to respect a little girl with no direction in life who turned a goat loose on a golf course?"

His comment hit too close to home. I was different. I

was only just now discovering my direction in life—and it scared me, but I didn't want to give him the satisfaction of bowing to his cruelty.

"The thing of it is, little girls grow into women who change the world. And right now, the world I'm planning on changing is yours."

He looked at me in shock. I picked up another chocolate covered strawberry and bit into it as I went in search of Noah.

No matter how I tried to block that man's words, I couldn't. I nodded as I passed a few people I'd met earlier in the evening.

Finally, I spotted him standing at the center of the display of minute paintings. Lottie was gracious enough to share—even though I quit the gallery.

Noah was talking with the woman I'd had the painting conversation with earlier that evening: the one who was interested in seeing more of my Picasso imitations. I knew it was only a matter of time before I met someone else who had impeccable artistry tastes came along.

As I approached Noah, he turned slightly towards me, not much, but enough that I noticed. He continued talking with the woman and two other gentlemen. As I studied the group, I knew deep down in my soul that Noah's grandpa was right. I didn't have what it took to mingle and pretend to be a wallflower. I didn't see myself as an extension of his business; I saw myself as someone who

Maybe I was too colorful for Noah. Maybe all the work at the golf course was an excuse to avoid me. He was such a gentleman that he probably didn't want to break up with me. He was too good of a guy. I was the one who kept pushing myself into his life. I couldn't do that to him anymore. I needed to give him the space he deserved. And

I deserved to be loved as much as I loved. Spending my time with someone who loved me less was a waste of time.

I couldn't compete with a golf course.

We'd seen so little of each other lately. Maybe he wanted to be done with our relationship. Maybe he didn't want to hurt my feelings by breaking up with me.

Chapter Twenty

NOAH

When Alec made his way over to the group I'd been speaking with, I was ready for what I knew was about to happen. His one goal in mind: to make himself look good and me look terrible. In his mind, he had an influential audience to woo. There were two bank owners: Paul Raglund and Gregory Toombs. My friend Xavier, a well-respected restaurateur, who had finally made it down to visit.

I knew to expect Grandfather's sharp tongue trying to make me look bad. What I hadn't expected was for Page to follow right on his heels.

Page slipped her hand underneath my elbow and leaned close to my side.

"Page, I'd like you to meet my good friend Xavier. This is Gregory Toombs, and this is Paul Raglund, Hagen's father."

"So nice to meet you all," Page smiled at each in turn. When she got to Paul, she reached a hand out to pat his arm. "My sincere condolences on your son marrying a Boone."

Paul leaned closer to her and lowered his voice. "I'll tell you a secret."

Page whispered loudly back at him. "I love secrets."

"I love my future daughter-in-law. I feel like it's against the rules of being an in-law, but I can't help but like Kylie, especially seeing her with Hagen."

Page grinned at him. "I think they're good for each other, too."

Grandfather's voice cut into their quiet conversation with his booming voice as he spoke to Gregory Toombs. Toombs ran the bank that held The Garden's last loan about to be paid.

"My grandson here is having trouble running a successful business. Dumb luck. I wish he would have inherited my sharp business sense," Alec was saying.

Page bristled next to me, "Remind me of the successful businesses you run? What are they again?"

I could have kissed her right then. Maybe put my hand over her mouth—anything to stop her from becoming his newest target.

Grandpa's face was turning red again, and he took a sip—gulp—of his wine before he answered her. "I've retired. No more running businesses for me. Now it's my turn to sit back while my grandson runs this place into bankruptcy."

"Funny you should say that because the course has reached a record high of members. Nearly double the amount there was when you were running it." Page laughed as though she were merely commenting on the color of his tie. "But, silly me, we're not here to talk business, we're here to drink wine and admire art."

She spun toward me and grabbed my hand. "Noah, there's a piece over there I wanted to show you."

She flashed a smile at my grandfather and his friends while I allowed her to pull me along.

"You're magnificent; you know that?"

She smiled, but it didn't reach her eyes. "I've thought that about myself before, so it's nice to have it confirmed."

"I saw my grandpa talking to you earlier. What did he say?"

"I would imagine it's his usual bluster."

"I'm sorry." I squeezed her hand as we stopped in front of an imitation Picasso.

"Why don't mine ever look like this?"

I shrugged, knowing it was best to keep my mouth shut. There is a time and a place for honesty, and this wasn't it.

"We've made the rounds enough, let's get out of here and grab some dinner by ourselves."

"That sounds like fun Noah, but I've got a headache."

That would explain why she was missing her regular sparkle. "Oh, no. I'm sorry. Let me lock my office then I'll drive you home."

She rested a hand on my arm. "No, it's okay. I'll drive myself home. All I need is to lay down and sleep. It will go away."

I studied her eyes. "You do look tired. I've been putting too much on you. You've been doing amazing with these art nights, but you're busy starting a business and running a coffee shop. You don't need more things to worry about."

"Noah. I'm okay, really. Just a headache. I'll talk to you later." She reached out and squeezed my arm before heading toward the lobby.

Grandpa had been busy.

It amazed me that one person could carry around so much bitterness for so long. I'd always heard that anger and resentment would eat away at a person. Not in Grandpa's case, he seemed to thrive on it. No matter. I'd learned a thing or two in my short life, and it would take more than my grandpa spreading lies to cause me to file for bankruptcy. I wasn't even going to acknowledge the rumors he'd started.

I'd paid off one of the loans then refinanced the remaining loans. It wouldn't take too much longer to pay those off, and then we would be entirely in the black. Toombs had been impressed with the art night and told me he'd be happy to work with me on the loan.

The next big thing was spring golf tournaments. We were planning a March golf tournament that would hopefully cement us as a reputable golf course in town.

I couldn't get a hold of Page the next morning. I'd shown up to the coffee shop to buy a cup of coffee—that I never ended up drinking—and she was busy taking inventory and couldn't come out from the back. Except when I walked back out to my car, I saw her face plastered to the window. Whatever the reason was that she was avoiding me, I would find out and fix it. Maybe I'd done something to make her mad. When I handed over all management duties to Kent, I planned on taking some time off to spend with Page. Of course, I had a few more business ideas I was throwing around in my head, but I would make sure they wouldn't interfere with how much time I wanted to spend with Page.

If I wanted to have a strong relationship with her, I needed to put the time and effort necessary for it. Maybe I was more like my grandfather than I thought—allowing the golf course to become the priority instead of relationships.

Chapter Twenty-One

PAGE

I went through the motions as I made my (yes, my) regulars' cups of coffee. I was so preoccupied that I didn't even remember to smile at my best tippers. I'd have to make it up to them in the future with an extra shot of coffee.

After I hid from Noah earlier that morning, I knew I had to make a decision—and fast. I couldn't keep avoiding him. And I couldn't keep feeling like he didn't love me as much as I loved him. It wasn't right. I wasn't a priority in his life.

"You're fired."

"Cletus, I'm not in the mood today."

Cletus leaned his cane against the counter. "Caroline isn't speaking to me."

"Hmm, no surprise there."

"It's your fault. You've been distracting her grandson, and now she feels like she needs to be there for him. I guess that lousy ex-husband of hers is causing problems."

"I don't doubt that for a second. I finally met him."

Cletus' eyes widened. "What was he like? Was he younger than me?"

"Cletus, everyone is younger than you. He was exactly how you would expect: self-absorbed and manipulative."

"What did he say?"

"He said I didn't belong with his grandson."

"He's not wrong."

"Thanks for the vote of confidence, Cletus."

"I mean it. I met some of Caroline's friends. It was a stuffy crowd."

I nodded. I knew what he meant.

"Maybe you and I are better off by ourselves."

"You might be right," I admitted. I knew I didn't fit in.

"Better lonely than stifled," Cletus grumbled.

"I'm not sure if that's true or not. I'll give it some thought, but right now, there's a line of people waiting for their coffees."

The next customer was a middle-aged woman with a cloud of hairspray preceding her. "Boyfriend trouble, honey?"

The sympathetic look on her face,

"It's just—I don't think he loves me as much as I love him."

"Did he tell you he loves you?" The woman asked.

"Well, yes."

"Then, he loves you."

"But he's too busy to spend time with me."

"Then, he probably doesn't love you." Another gentleman sitting at a small table close by added. "Men will make time for what's important to them."

I sipped my iced coffee. "Good point. He's an amazing guy. I love him. But I don't know if I should stay with him if he doesn't feel the same way."

Another woman, Tasha, a regular, came to stand by the

counter next to me. "If he loves you, then he'll make an effort."

"That's what I thought."

"Maybe he's just reserved!" Mitchell, the blogger who came into the shop every day, piped up. He quickly buried his face behind his laptop again.

"Mitchell's got a point," Tasha agreed. "Maybe he doesn't know how to make an effort?"

Edward, Cletus' chess partner, walked over to the counter. The man rested a hand against the glass pastry shelf. "My wife says I should keep my hands to myself more often."

I snagged the cleaning spray and a rag and walked around to the outside of the counter. "Excuse me."

The man moved his hand, and I sprayed the finger-prints with the cleaner. "My boyfriend keeps his hands to himself. That's not the problem."

I finished polishing the glass.

Edward spoke up, "When I was young, men weren't scared to say it like it is."

I nodded as I reached up and pulled Edward's thick glasses off his face, quickly polishing them with my rag before I set them back on the end of his nose.

"Your man might just need to have a chat with one of us old-timers to learn how it's done."

"You're probably right, Edward."

"Does he kiss you?"

I'm not sure who asked. "Well, he kisses me back when I kiss him."

A collective groan went throughout the room.

"He hasn't initiated it?"

"I, uh, well, not nearly as often as me."

I looked around at the sympathetic looks on their faces. That was when I realized something.

I was a pity girlfriend.

I'd barged into Noah's life and commandeered it. Maybe he thought he loved me simply because I hadn't given him a chance to think otherwise. Now that he knew he didn't love me, he probably wasn't sure how to break the news to me.

I think I felt my heart physically split down the middle at the thought. I couldn't swallow.

I knew what I had to do.

I had to set him free.

Knowing what you have to do, and doing it, are two very different things.

I knew I couldn't be a pity girlfriend. I knew I couldn't even be a second thought girlfriend. I needed to be a priority. I'd been on the back burner with my parents ever since the twins were born. I didn't want to spend the rest of my life with someone who would treated me the same way.

When I parked my car at the golf course parking lot, I slipped inside through the caddy entrance. I didn't want to have to stop and chat with Alisha or Mandy. Or worse, see Kent and have to explain why I was there. After peeking through a few doors, I headed upstairs. Noah needed to add some security to the club. It wasn't tough to sneak past everyone.

When I finally found Noah in his office upstairs, he looked surprised to see me.

"I think we need to take a break," I blurted out.

"You're right. We've been spending way too much time here. I'm sorry."

I bit my lip. "That's not what I meant, Noah."

He stopped sorting through the papers on his desk.

"What are you saying, Page?"

"I'm saying we need to stop dating."

"What? Why?" He stood up and leaned his hands on the desk. His eyes were hard as he studied my face.

Okay, scary-Noah was making a reappearance. I wasn't sure I could face him right then.

"You and I are so different, you know?"

He shook his head. "Of course, I know that. We're incredibly different."

I smiled with quivering lips. Darn those tears trying to sneak out. "The novelty will wear off. And where will that leave me? Broken-hearted." Ha. I'm such a faker; I was already broken-hearted.

"You're ending our relationship based on what could happen?" He walked around the desk and stopped in front of me, where he shoved his hands in his pockets.

"Don't make this harder than it is. You're an amazing man, Noah. I've had a great time with you. But all good things come to an end."

"But I thought you—"

His stormy eyes nearly shattered me.

"I'll see you around, Noah."

Then I ran—like the coward I was—down the stairs. I barely dodged Kent in the hall, my vision blurry as tears streamed down my face.

All I wanted was to curl up in a ball and look up travel plans that I couldn't afford.

I couldn't see Noah again. I was too weak. If I saw him, I'd leap into his arms and wrap around him like a boa constrictor. He'd have to peel me off like Velcro.

That's why I chose the coward's way—a break-up and run. I couldn't stay and talk it out. I would lose my resolve —and my self-respect.

I called Jenny immediately after breaking up with Noah, and demanded that she meet me at my house with a box of beignets and chocolate milk.

I lay on my back on my fluffy rug, staring at the ceiling, waiting for some grand epiphany to hit me. Waiting for my life's purpose to come drifting towards me, Mary Poppins style. Instead, all I saw floating towards me was dust and heartache.

The door shook when someone knocked on it. I must have laid on that rug for a long time because there was only one person in the world who knocked like that.

"Come in!" I yelled.

Jenny marched inside, carrying two paper sacks. "What's the occasion?"

"I broke up with Noah."

"Huh. That's a shame. I actually liked him." She sat down on my bed and opened the bag. She pulled out a beignet and bit it in half. Jenny didn't belong in the south with her uncouth manners, but it was something that made her fun—relatable even—though we didn't dare say it out loud. Our parents would kill us. Every family has a black sheep and Jenny's ours. She was well-loved by all of us cousins, though.

"Jenny, I don't want to talk about it."

"Thank goodness; I don't either." She popped the cap off a bottle of chocolate milk and passed it to me.

"But I'm going to anyway."

She glared at me. "I'm going to kill you."

"You wish. I think you're just upset that I was the one to kill Lucifer."

She nodded slowly. "Maybe. All right, I'll give you ten minutes. Whine and complain about your boyfriend, and then I don't want to hear another word."

It was the best offer I'd ever get from someone like Jenny.

"I love him. I wanted it to work out, but I guess you can't change that we're from different worlds."

"Does he have a bunch of money or something?"

"No, the golf course was close to bankruptcy when he took over. He's not a snob, if that's what you mean," I defended him.

Jenny held up her hands in a surrender motion, "I was just trying to figure out why you ended things."

"It's just that the world he's in is so, stuck up. Rule following. Traditional."

"So you're saying his world is snobby, but he isn't?"

I opened my mouth then closed it. "Well, yes, I guess so. It's just when we've been hosting the art and golf nights. I feel so out of place. Then that cantankerous old man told me I was too fresh for that scene and that Noah would never gain traction in the business world with me at his side. I quote, 'you're too colorful.'"

"Well, where does he live? I'm going to have to kill the man now. Who is he?"

"Noah's grandfather."

Jenny picked up another beignet and shoved it in her mouth. "Well, didn't you say that Noah inherited this golf course from the grandpa?"

"Well, yes. But what does that have to do with it?" I took a drink of the too-sweet chocolate milk.

"Oh, nothing, I'm just trying to get a clear picture of what's going on with you and Noah."

"Stop trying to figure it out and sympathize with me. He spent all his time at the golf course. I wasn't a priority in his life. I think maybe all that work was an excuse to avoid me."

"Are you sure you're not projecting?"

"Of course not!" I snapped at her. "You're projecting.

It was going to be a long evening…

Chapter Twenty-Two

NOAH

I don't know how long I sat in my chair staring at my computer screen. It's what I'd been doing for an entire week.

Shocked. I didn't see this coming. I thought we were fine. Heck, I loved her. I'd even told her. I'd had a ring made specifically for her.

"Boss. Everything okay?" Kent asked as he stepped inside my office.

"Peachy."

"So…I wouldn't ask normally, but I passed Page in the hall a week ago when she was running and crying. I didn't know she was capable of crying. And now you've been worthless ever since."

I glanced up sharply. "You didn't tell me you'd seen her. What did she say to you?"

He shrugged. "Nothing. As I said, she was running out crying."

I slammed my fist into my desktop. If she truly wanted to break up with me, why would she be so hurt by it? I was going to figure it out. I couldn't—wouldn't—believe that she was happy to break up with me. There had to be something more at play here.

"I've got to figure out what happened."

"I know what happened."

Kent and I spun around to stare at Jenny standing in the office doorway, holding a nine-iron.

"Jenny. I thought you were in Oregon."

"Not yet. I couldn't exactly leave when Page has been a blubbering mess on my couch."

"You know what happened?"

"Your grandpa sabotaged you." She strode into the office, tapping the club along the ground like a cane.

"Yes, I know, we figured out about the bribing last week. He's been trying to tank this business ever since he handed it over."

Jenny tapped the golf club against my desk. "That's not what I meant. He planted the seed of doubt in Page's mind."

I sighed. "Whatever he planted in her mind shouldn't have had a chance to grow if she was really giving us a chance."

"Okay, so maybe she watered and fertilized it. But she needs you." Jenny thumped the club against the desk a little harder. Kent jumped where he stood by the door.

"Hey, knock that off, you'll dent the wood. It might be the only genuine piece of furniture in this office, and I need it to last." I ran my hand over the surface but couldn't feel a scratch.

"Your grandfather told her that you needed someone more serious at your side if you're going to be successful as this golf course and as a businessman."

"My grandpa wouldn't know a successful businessman if he were introduced to one—and he has been."

"Amen to that," Kent muttered as he sat down in a chair next to my bay window.

"Oh, I know that. And you know that. But Page wants the best for you. I mean," Jenny paused and stifled a yawn with her hand, "she even loves you. That's why she's sacrificing her feelings."

I stood up. "I knew it. What a ridiculous idea!"

"Sit down. Let me tell you something about Page. You can't tell her something just once; you need to tell her over and over again. Then you need to keep on telling it to her. She needs spontaneity and affection. She's pretty much like a cat. When was the last time you initiated a hug?"

"We hug all the time."

I tried to recall our movie marathon nights and every date we went on. It wasn't hard to do. Every occasion was pressed firmly into my memory. "Well, I guess she instigated most of it."

"Exactly. She thinks her love for you is one-sided. Page thrives on affection. You have to tell her you love her constantly, hold her hand, kiss her in public, and she'd probably follow you off a cliff."

"Me specifically or anyone she treated this way?"

"You, you thick-headed—"

I waved her off. "Okay, I think I get the general idea." Frustrated with myself that I hadn't realized it before. Page *was* very affectionate. It was one of the many things I loved about her. She wasn't afraid to show her love for someone.

"What are you going to do about it?"

"I'm going to go order the biggest cup of coffee, tip like crazy, and tell her I love her."

"Not good enough."

"What?"

"Come on, where's your grand gesture? You can't just

waltz in there and pretend like a few words will solve everything."

"Why not?"

She looked at me as if I was the biggest idiot on the face of the earth.

"Knock-knock," Mack called from the open doorway.

"Oh good, you're here. Come talk some sense into him," Jenny said as Mack entered the office.

"What's going on?" Mack asked as he sat in the leather chair that faced out the big bay window.

I walked over to stand next to the window and looked out over the course. It was almost as if I could still see Page napping on the green like the first day I laid eyes on her.

"She broke up with me."

"Yes, I know. It's been a week. The news is all over the family," Mack answered. "What are you going to do about it?"

"Do about it? What is with you Boones? Why can't I go grovel and ask her out again?"

"Because she's a Boone. Even more important, she's Page. If you want her attention, you'll have to play by her terms. She wants unconditional love."

Jenny flopped into the empty leather seat next to Mack's.

"She's got my unconditional love."

They said nothing, just kept staring out the window.

"She's amazing to be around; she brightens every room she walks in. She's always showing me affection. She's even always trying to fix my problems for me. She's the best thing that ever happened to me. How could she not know I adore her?"

Neither of them answered me.

"Crap."

"On a stick," Jenny added.

"She's been doing all the work in our relationship, hasn't she?"

"Yup," Mack answered.

I'd assumed she knew. I'd thought I was clear with my love for her. I had to find out exactly where I'd messed up. "Okay. You two. You're going to help me figure something out to make this up to her."

Jenny's smile turned positively evil. Maybe asking them for help wasn't one of my better ideas.

Kent groaned. "You're asking this one for ideas? That's a bad idea, Noah."

Jenny pointed the golf club at Kent, who immediately closed his mouth. She turned back to face me. "I think you should kidnap her."

"No," Mack shook his head. "Too illegal. She might kill you. You should just ask her to marry you."

Jenny frowned at him. "She'd kill him if he did that right after she broke up with him."

The two of them continued to argue about my grand gesture, and I pulled out a cigarette from my pocket. I didn't even care if it was against code to smoke in my office. I needed a cigarette. Before I brought it to my lips, something knocked it out of my hands. Jenny stood there with the golf club pointed at me. "I promised Page I wouldn't let you take up smoking again."

"She told you about that?"

"Yes, while she was sobbing into a chocolate milk container because her 'life was over.' She wanted to make sure someone still took care of you."

"She could have taken care of me herself!"

"I know. But Page doesn't see it that way. She wants you to marry someone you truly love. She's convinced herself you weren't very serious about her."

I groaned as I opened another can of iced tea instead.

I'd consumed more caffeine the last week than should be humanly possible. The longer I was away from Page, the harder it got. I was getting desperate. I needed a Page fix.

"Of course, I love her! Who did she think was taking her on all those dates these past couple months? Who was getting ready to give up his business so he could travel the world with her?" I couldn't stop the rant once I started.

"Oh no," Jenny muttered. "He's talking about himself in the third person."

"You've done it now. I've never seen him mad before." Mack eyed me warily. Well, they were the ones who barged into my office, so if they saw me unhinged, it was their own fault.

"Who tried to support her with her design business? Who told her she should travel wherever she wanted—with a friend? Who bought her a ring and wanted to spend the rest of his life with her?"

Someone gasped. I wasn't sure which of them—probably Mack.

"He bought her a ring," Mack coughed out.

"Well, if you want a finger to put that ring on, you better make sure she knows what you think," Jenny goaded.

"Pushy, pushy," Kent mumbled loud enough for us to hear.

I nodded at him before I responded to Jenny. "Don't think I don't realize you're trying to get me to do something incredibly stupid like show up at her work and kidnap her."

Jenny shook her head rapidly and made a poor imitation of an innocent face. "I would never!"

"Good. It's not going to happen. I'll explain it to her over dinner like a civilized person. There will be no kidnapping, or drastic anything. And that's final."

Chapter Twenty-Three

PAGE

I messed up five orders in a row and cried when I made a coffee for a girl named Nola because it sounded similar to Noah. I dropped a gallon of milk and forgot all the regular customers' coffee orders.

Time was not healing all hurt. I was getting more obsessive over it. It wasn't getting easier. I knew I made the right choice. I only wished that would help me sleep at night.

I was well on my way to becoming the next meme of a klutzy girl. Cletus relegated me to cardboard duty. It was glamorous. It involved a box cutter, minimal folding skills, and expert level stacking. Once the stack got too high, then it had to be carried out of the back room and into the recycle bin behind the shop. I was preparing to take the first load of five hundred and forty trips when Cletus stepped in front of me.

"You really liked that fancy fella, didn't you?"

I stamped my foot and glared at the wrinkles next to his eyes. "Yes, Cletus. I liked that 'fella,' as you call him. He was wonderful. But I just didn't belong in his world, and he didn't love me as much as I loved him."

"You sure about that? I saw you two together. He looked plenty happy having you on his arm."

"Cletus, where are you going with this? Just the other day, you told me we were better off without Noah and Caroline."

"Since when have you ever listened to anything someone told you to do? If he asked you to marry him, would you?"

"If he meant it. If he loved me as much as I love him, I would in a heartbeat."

"Well, good."

"But, he doesn't."

"What makes you say that?"

"I'm not a priority. He doesn't like to be around me as much as I like to be around him. We come from different worlds. His is very proper. Mine is fairly carefree. He doesn't know how to bend the rules—he has to succeed in his mind."

"You mean he's no fun."

"If he's not willing to risk anything for me, that means he doesn't care for me."

I was getting tired of the conversation, and I needed to add the cardboard to the recycle bin out back.

"Well, I think he's about to change your mind," Cletus muttered as I walked past him and grabbed the door. I glanced at him over my shoulder.

"What are you talking about?"

"Oh, nothing." He waved me away and headed back towards the front of the coffee shop. He really was a strange one. If he didn't need me so much, I'd up and quit with all his nosiness.

I opened the door and dragged the folded boxes

outside. Setting them down, I closed the door after myself. We didn't want to leave the door open too long; Cletus and I hated to overwork the air conditioner.

I turned around again to grab the boxes but came face to face with a chest. I glanced up and met Noah's stormy eyes.

"What—what are you doing here?" *Excellent work playing the calm and collected ex-girlfriend, Page.*

"I'm here to make sure you can't walk away from me again."

I had no idea what he meant. Obviously, he wasn't here to kill me; at least I knew that much about him. "What's it to be? Dumped in the river or the dumpster?"

"Something even better," he said as he leaned forward and wrapped an arm around my waist and started dragging me off toward the back of the parking lot.

"Noah, knock it off, I have to get back to work." I dug my heels in, but he lifted me off my feet. His arms wrapped around my waist and he held me off the ground. My chest pressed against his chest, my legs dangling against his.

"Those boxes aren't going to break themselves down, you know," I told him, even though I didn't care one bit about those boxes. Good riddance. Noah was holding me. It was unconventional, but he was holding me. Maybe it was *because* it was unconventional that I liked it. It had been a long week without him.

Noah's arms tightened around me. All right, it was unconventional, but I had tips to make inside, and false hope was a devil. "Seriously, Noah put me down. I refuse to be the next Lucifer at your golf course."

"I don't want to share you with anyone, but I'm sure if you were our mascot, we would have more club members than any other golf course in the world." He stopped walking and stood there looking at me, my feet still dangling a foot above the ground. "Actually, that's a wonderful idea. I'll have to tell Kent. He'll love the idea. We could make t-shirts with your face on them. They would read, 'I survived Page.'"

I smacked his chest and tried to knee him in the side, but it wasn't easy to do when he held me tight against his chest. "What do you want, Noah? You let me go already. I don't know what you're doing here. And why are you carrying me?"

He pressed his lips together, and it looked as though he were planning his answer. "Okay. Yes, I let you go, but that was the biggest mistake of my life. I want you."

I studied his chocolate eyes. "An even bigger mistake than taking on that golf course?"

He nodded and adjusted his hold around my waist, "It was an even bigger mistake than taking over that golf course. As for what I'm doing here, that should be obvious."

"You're trying to strain your back by holding me too long?"

"No, this is my grand gesture." With a big grin, he took off across the parking lot at a brisk pace, our legs knocking together with every step he took.

"What's the grand gesture? Showing me how strong you are?" I reached my arms around his neck and held tight. It felt so good to be touching him again. He wanted me. Whatever this grand gesture thing was that he was talking about, at least now I knew he wanted me. We could work out all the details later; it didn't matter to me.

"I'm kidnapping you." He grinned as a sleek black SUV pulled to a stop next to us.

He set me down and opened the door. "After you."

"Wait. I'm not getting in that car until you tell me what

you have planned." I said. I wanted to see know how far he was willing to take this grand gesture of his.

He clenched his jaw and nodded as he met my gaze. "Well, then."

I yelped as he scooped me off my feet bridal-carry style and set me into the car. He climbed in after me and slammed the door. The doors locked immediately after.

He'd done it. He'd picked me up and shoved me into a car.

"You... you..." I couldn't think of anything to call him. He was breaking the rules, he was trying to show me he loved me. He was acting without thought. He was acting like—well, like me. "You kidnapped me!"

He grinned at me. "Yeah, I did. I've been wanting to sweep you off your feet ever since I met you. Maybe I should have kidnapped you that first day."

"That would have saved me a lot of trouble." A voice said from the front seat. I hadn't even thought to look at who was driving the car. I'd been so focused on Noah and pushing him beyond his boundaries.

"Well, if it isn't Clark Kent, the professional kidnapper." I met his eyes in the rearview mirror. He held up a roll of duct tape and waved it around.

"Here, Noah, we're prepared. I don't want to have to listen to her whining the whole way there."

I leaned forward and flicked the back of his ear.

"Ouch, wow, real mature, Pager-pager."

Noah snatched me back to his side before I could launch a full assault on the driver. I turned and pressed my face against Noah's chest. He smelled so good. I'd missed his smell in the week we'd been apart. I ran my hand back and forth across his abdomen just to reassure myself that he was really here, that he was holding me.

"So, your grand gesture is to torture me by making me ride with Superman?"

"Yes, I asked myself; what's the sure way to make sure she spends the rest of her life with me? Then I realized that if you spent some time in Kent's company, I would seem like the better option." He whisper-yelled loud enough for Kent to hear.

I laughed, "You're right, that could push me into anyone's arms, though."

Noah smiled and leaned his head down to kiss my forehead while he stroked my hair gently. "We're going on a trip."

"What?"

"We're taking a week off. Kent's dropping us off at the airport."

He was being spontaneous—for me. "I didn't ask for time off."

"I called and talked with Cletus. You have time off. We'll be back before you have any spring decorating to do."

I hated taking care of pesky details, like managing dates and work schedules. And going on a trip with him sounded wonderful. "You're the most beautiful man I've ever seen."

"I keep telling you to get your eyes checked," he teased.

"Wait—you said Kent's taking us to the airport? As in, right now? Right this minute?"

Noah smiled and nodded.

I sat up and smacked his chest, "I don't have my purse or any clothes. Turn around and give me a little while to pack."

Noah raised his eyebrows at me. "Please give me a little more credit than that. Cletus brought me your purse and phone, and Jenny packed a suitcase with everything you'll need in it."

I bit my lip to keep from laughing. He even had that planned down to the last detail. "Well, thanks, and I think I need to have some words with Cletus about going behind my back. And just wait until I get my hands on Jenny. She has the worst fashion sense I've ever seen. If you think I'm going to wear the clothes she packed—"

I didn't get another word out, because Noah's lips were pressed against mine, stealing my breath away. He held my head in place with one hand while he slowly explored my lips.

As if I'd try to get away. I loved his kisses, and I intended to kiss him as much as humanly possible. We would become record breakers for the longest-lasting kiss.

"Get a room!" Kent called from the front seat.

"Now can I kill him?" I asked Noah. I'd been so lost in our kiss that I didn't know how long we'd sat there tangled together. I would gladly use my golf club on Kent right then.

"We need him to take us to the airport."

"Where are we going?"

He smiled knowingly at me. "It's a surprise. Jenny was pretty sure you'd like it. She said you'd like the whole grand-gesture kidnapping thing too."

"You mean to tell me that you believed Jenny when she told you to kidnap me?" I couldn't imagine him being swayed by someone. And I think the fact that he was willing to go to such lengths to show me that he cared was the true grand gesture. Forget kidnapping.

"I suggested an empty warehouse where you could dump the body," Kent suggested helpfully.

I ignored him, and Noah did too because he closed the distance between us and wrapped both his arms around my shoulders and kissed me like he meant it. He kissed me like he wasn't going to let me go. He kissed me like he didn't want a stuffy girlfriend.

"I have one favor to ask."

"Okay." I licked my lips. He'd left a hint of cinnamon behind.

"Please don't hang anymore of your Picasso paintings in the club."

"My Picassos aren't that bad. I mean, I've seen worse in art galleries."

"We're here!" Kent interrupted my defense of my paintings as he stopped the car in the drop-off zone at the airport.

"You need to tell me where we are going since you kidnapped me," I told him as he helped me out of the car. I loved what a gentleman he was. I also loved that he thought it was a good idea to kidnap me. He opened the rear trunk and pulled out two large suitcases.

"What are those for?"

He smiled at me. "Our trip."

"Oh no, Jenny probably packed everything we don't need. She probably forgot to add any clothes or anything useful."

Noah set down the suitcases and grabbed my chin. He stared into my eyes. I wondered if he realized there were other people on the sidewalk next to us. Public displays of affection weren't his thing.

He leaned closer until our breath mingled. "What is it?"

"I love you, Page, you swung your way into my life. I want you in my life. I'm sorry you ever doubted my love for you. I'm sorry my actions made you doubt that love. Please don't leave me again. My heart can't take it."

"Try and make me."

"It's because of you, I've started to feel at peace again. You've reminded me how to enjoy the moment, not always rush forward because we have to stay on a schedule. Because of you, I started willingly taking time off of work. Because of you, I've began reconnecting with my sister. You've reminded me what's important in life. With your help, I'm going to continue living in the moment."

I reached up and gently brushed my fingers against his cheek. "There is no one else like you Noah. And you're all mine. Now, where are we going?"

His smile stretched from ear to ear. "We're getting married in Vegas."

I choked on the cinnamon gum in my mouth. I tried to suck in a breath, but my lungs seemed to have collapsed. "What did you say?" I wheezed.

"We're getting married in Vegas."

"That's what I thought you said." I shook my head. "You haven't even asked me."

"I love you. You love me. We both want to spend the rest of our lives together, so let's do that." He pulled something out of his pocket and slipped it onto my finger.

It was a rose-gold band-shaped and designed like roses and leaves leading up to a brown diamond. It was gorgeous and unique — no solitaire diamond for me.

"Where did you find this?"

He raised his eyebrows. "I had it made a month after we started dating. I knew you were the one for me. I was hanging onto it for just the right time, but you've pushed me too far this time. You don't get to wait until our first dating anniversary—you get it now."

"This is—" I held my hand up in the air and studied it. There was a beautiful ring on my finger—on my ring finger. The man wanted to marry me—marry me that weekend. "Well, I guess I have to marry you now. This ring is too pretty to part with."

I shrugged as if I weren't trying to stop gaping at it.

He grinned at me. "You realize you're waving at everyone who walks into the airport right now."

I glanced around and noticed people staring at my raised hand. "Oh well. Let them look. They can see exactly what an engagement ring should look like."

He grinned and shoved his hands in his pockets.

"You're always shoving your hands in your pockets! Is it a nervous habit?"

"Want to know why?" he growled.

Oh, this was new. He leaned towards me. "I had to keep my hands occupied and away from you, or I would do this."

He was so fast I didn't even see him move. He grabbed me around my waist and yanked me against his chest. Then his hands were plundering my hair, his lips pressed against my mouth, kissing me to the depths of my soul.

When he finally pulled away, I was breathless.

"That's why I keep my hands in my pockets."

I licked my lips. "I'm going to have to buy you some pocketless pants because that wasn't so bad."

"One more comment like that—"

He didn't get to finish, because I reached up and pulled his mouth back to mine. Two could play this game.

He pulled back and smiled at me. "We're getting married."

I locked my hands together behind his waist. "You realize that getting married doesn't just automatically fix our problems, right?"

Noah leaned down and kissed my forehead. "I know. But I want to spend the rest of my life with you—problems and all. I'm trying to show you how much I care about you and love you."

"How does marrying me prove that?"

"It's not the marrying that proves that—it's the part that follows."

I waggled my eyebrows.

He smirked, "Not that. I meant we're traveling."

"What?"

"You and I are traveling. Going abroad. Taking a vacation. Going on holiday. Take your pick. We're doing it. We're going to make our businesses fit around our traveling schedule. I'm going to spend my life showing you how much I love you and how much you matter to me."

"You're taking a break from your routine and business for me?"

"You matter to me. This relationship isn't going to just be us hanging around The Garden. I don't want to wake up one day and realize that all I've done is work and ignore the most amazing woman in the world. From now on, *you* are my priority."

I sighed, "And you'll always been mine."

EPILOGUE

Noah

"*Y*ou beat me to it."

I spun around to find Hagen standing behind me in his black tux, his hair styled for once. It even looked like he'd shaved his stubble for the day.

The day.

The day Kylie and Page had been freaking out about for a couple of months now.

Kylie and Hagen's wedding day.

"What exactly did I beat you at?" I straightened my jacket sleeve. "There have been so many things."

Hagen laughed. "Oh, that's funny. I was telling you that you beat me at something because I wanted you to have at least one success in your life."

"I'm still not sure what you're talking about, but you look like you've never tied a tie before." I dropped my phone in my pocket. Kent had texted to let me know everything had been fine at the golf course over the last month.

Hagen's hand shot up to his neck and patted the limp, crooked bow tie. "It's not that bad, is it?"

I nodded.

With a groan, he pulled it loose and set about retying it. Each attempt was worse than the last.

"What was it I won?" I asked.

"You got married first. Thank goodness Kylie isn't one of those petty people. Because I know it would upset some women about their cousin eloping only a short while before their wedding."

I couldn't stand watching his bumbling hands anymore. I knocked them out of the way and quickly tied the bow knot.

"I don't know why I'm so nervous. Were you this nervous?"

I nodded and straightened the tie one last time. "I thought I was going to end up in a heap at Elvis's feet."

Hagen chuckled at that. Yes, it had been an Elvis wedding. Page had been so excited she acted like we were getting married in Buckingham Palace.

"It's just—Kylie's something else. I'm scared she'll wake up and realize she could have done better than me."

Shaking my head, I glanced around the corner and down the hall.

Page exited a room a few doors down.

I stepped away from the doorway and turned to answer him. "You know, if she hasn't come to her senses by now, she probably never will. You're in luck."

Hagen snorted. "Thanks for the pep talk."

"Anytime."

Page stepped around the corner, wearing a pale-yellow dress. Her hair was twisted together somehow and draped over her shoulder. She smiled and reached up to tug me down by my lapels. She kissed me soundly, then pulled back. "You look good in black."

"You look good in no—" She kissed me again to cut off what I was going to say. Something I'd learned in our short time together as a married couple: it was possible to embarrass her.

"Look what you've done. You've crushed my collar." I pretended to be offended as I pushed her away. "Keep your hands to yourself, woman. There's an unmarried child present."

We glance at Hagen, who was busy wiping his sweaty palms against his pants.

"Oh, don't mind me. I think I'll go down the hall and revisit my breakfast." Hagen dashed out of the room, looking a little pale.

"Quit picking on Hagen. Besides, I left a wrapped Picasso imitation on the gift table."

I pulled her tight against me, relieved that she'd finally realized imitation painting wasn't her strong suit. "You're right. I have much more important things to do than harass Hagen on his wedding day."

"Oh, you do?" Page bit her bottom lip. "And what is that exactly?"

"Kiss my wife."

The END

ACKNOWLEDGMENTS

Thank you for reading Friends Like These!
This was a fun and unusual story to write, thanks to
Grandpa Jim.
My Grandpa used to tell me stories all the time: most of
them were snake stories. Since he grew up around the
swamps and bayous, he had a lot of run-ins with big ugly
snakes. Now, I'm not sure how much was true, or how
much was just a "snake story" but my Grandpa imparted a
love of stories to me at a young age. That is something I
will be forever grateful for!

I hope you enjoyed Page and Noah's story and that it made
you smile, or even better—ugly laugh.
There's nothing I love quite as much as making people
smile.
Here's to smiling at the odd, strange, humorous things that
happen in our daily lives!

Neighbors Like That

KYLIE
He started our war—I intend to finish it.

Buying a house in the suburbs was supposed to be low stress: my own little haven to decorate and landscape exactly how I want. Instead I find myself locking my garbage can to keep pests out—pests that are six-foot-one, green-eyed, and far too good looking.
My trespassing neighbor is rude and entitled. It isn't long before war is declared and I find myself stooping to immature pranks.
When trouble lands at my door, my unlikely neighbor starts knocking on my heart. Was I ready to answer?

HAGEN
I will win no matter what it takes.

I moved to this neighborhood for a fresh start. The one

thing I'm not looking for is a relationship, so when I mistakenly assume my neighbor is hitting on me, I lash out at her.

I didn't mean to start the war, but now she taunts me from across the street. Our harmless pranks have become the highlight of my day. I should stay away–but I can't. I want to spend more time with her.

When a stalker begins sending Kylie a series of notes, I'm only too willing to help protect her.

Maybe I'm looking for a relationship after all.

CHRISTMAS LIKE THIS

MARLA

I know exactly what I'd like to put in Trey's stocking: the
biggest lump of coal I can carry.
Unfortunately, I won't get the chance, because our boss has
delivered an ultimatum: plan the company Christmas party
with Trey and learn to get along, or else.
After only one day of trying to plan the Christmas party,
I'm ready to pick the "or else." Is it possible to learn to get
along with the most aggravating, overprotective, handsome
guy I've ever known?
We're about to find out if we can get our names off the
naughty list or not.